# "Here's what I want you to do,"

Devlin said. "When they come back, you say you know nothing. Be convincing. *Very* convincing."

Mackenzie spoke tentatively. "What if I don't want to—"

He was fast. Before she could blink, Devlin was standing in front of her, dragging her close against his chest. The move was supposed to be intimidating—and it was—but the great threat was the way he made her feel.

*Alive.* Scared, but so incredibly alive.

"You'll do it," he said grittily.

"Or what?"

Devlin's lips came down on hers, knocking out every objection with one striking blow. His mouth was hot and his tongue was wicked. The shock was staggering. Mackenzie hadn't known that a kiss could be so savage and still turn her molten with desire.

He wrenched his mouth away.

Mackenzie was paralyzed, swaying on her frozen feet. "Or what?" was all she could think to say.

"Or I'll never kiss you like that again."

Dear Reader,

I sum up this book in five words: Bad Boy Goes
Willie Wonka.

Does a tough-guy hero like Devlin Brandt have the same
sexy charisma if he's wearing rather outlandish seventies
garb instead of a leather jacket and jeans? What if he's
hiding out from the bad guys by working behind the
counter at a penny-candy store? In *Sinfully Sweet*,
Mackenzie, the youngest Bliss sister, discovers that
her old high-school crush on Devlin is still going strong.
And she just might have a few surprises of her own up
her sleeve...or in her candy dish!

If you enjoyed Sabrina Bliss's story in *The Chocoloate
Seduction* (Temptation #925), I think you're ready for
another wild ride into the world of SEX & CANDY.
Indulge!

Carrie Alexander

P.S. Don't forget to stop by my Web site at
www.carriealexander.com to sign up for my SEX &
CANDY giveaways. And drop me a note while you're
there—I'd love to hear from you.

## Books by Carrie Alexander

### HARLEQUIN TEMPTATION
839—SMOOTH MOVES
869—RISKY MOVES
925—THE CHOCOLATE
    SEDUCTION*

### HARLEQUIN BLAZE
20—PLAYING WITH FIRE

### HARLEQUIN SUPERROMANCE
1042—THE MAVERICK
1102—NORTH COUNTRY MAN

### HARLEQUIN DUETS
25—CUSTOM-BUILT COWBOY
32—COUNTERFEIT COWBOY
38—KEEPSAKE COWBOY
83—ONCE UPON A TIARA**
    —HENRY EVER AFTER**

*Sex & Candy
**Red-Hot Royals

# Sinfully Sweet
## Carrie Alexander

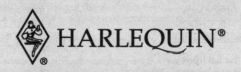

### HARLEQUIN®

TORONTO • NEW YORK • LONDON
AMSTERDAM • PARIS • SYDNEY • HAMBURG
STOCKHOLM • ATHENS • TOKYO • MILAN • MADRID
PRAGUE • WARSAW • BUDAPEST • AUCKLAND

ISBN 0-373-69129-7

SINFULLY SWEET

Copyright © 2003 by Carrie Antilla.

This edition published by arrangement with Harlequin Books S.A.

® and TM are trademarks of the publisher. Trademarks indicated with ® are registered in the United States Patent and Trademark Office, the Canadian Trade Marks Office and in other countries.

Visit us at www.eHarlequin.com

**Printed in U.S.A.**

# Prologue

"I AM GOING TO DO IT," Mackenzie Bliss said with all the bravado she could muster.

Sabrina glanced at her with an easy nonchalance. "You don't *have* to do it."

*Everything comes easy to Sabrina,* Mackenzie thought, taking in her sister's sloppy appearance. In a denim skirt and a sleeveless ribbed T-shirt that showed her flat tummy, Sabrina still managed to look good. Whereas Mackenzie had groomed herself for an hour and felt like potatoes stuffed into a designer gunnysack.

"I'm not going to force you." Sabrina squinted into the distance, avoiding her sister's eyes.

Mackenzie knew why. Sabrina was hoping that *she'd* fail first. If their bet was off, Sabrina would be free to pursue the gorgeous chocolate chef, Kit Rex.

"Hmm," Mackenzie said as if she were thinking about bailing. It was only to torture her sister, who was one year older but didn't often act like it. "Ah— no. I'm definitely going through with this."

"All right, but then we have to go inside, don't we?"

They stood near the glass double doors of a glam Madison Avenue salon. It was the type of place Mackenzie used to walk by with a guilty speed, as if the stylists might be standing in the window, rating the bad haircuts and fashion faux pas of the rabble who couldn't afford their services.

"Hold on, hold on. I'm thinking about it." Mackenzie adjusted the wide belt slung around her hips. A personal shopper at Barneys had sworn the belt enhanced her shape without actually drawing attention to its healthy proportions. An impossibility, in retrospect.

Sabrina had finally grown frustrated. "Really, Mackenzie, this is ridiculous. Get in there. It's only hair, not an arm or a leg. *Nothing* to be nervous about."

"Says you." Mackenzie pulled her waist-length braid over one shoulder, feeling protective now that she was on the verge of cutting it off. Sabrina also had long hair, but she hadn't even combed hers, just dragged it up into a messy ponytail. She was gorgeous nonetheless, although her looks weren't very important to her. She'd probably shave her head on a whim.

The difference was that Sabrina didn't need the reassurance. She had an interesting character, a striking face and a skinny model's body, while Mackenzie was quiet, even shy, and a model-size twelve. She'd grown comfortable with her shape—most of the time—but avoided being the center of attention if she could, unlike her sister. Why Mackenzie had agreed to a bet that made her exactly that was a mystery as great as the Pyramids.

Two months ago, Mackenzie and Sabrina's parents had remarried after having been divorced for sixteen years. The wedding had been a catalyst for the sisters to examine how they'd let their parents' breakup misshape their lives. Swept up in the air of romance and possibility, they'd challenged each other to change, to find their own true happiness. Sabrina had even put up stakes—the heirloom diamond ring that had been passed down to her on the eve of their parents' wedding. Their mother had chosen to start off fresh with a ring that hadn't already been through a divorce.

Suddenly, the challenge had become a bet. Sabrina, the wanderer without a committed bone in her body, was to try settling down for the first time in her life. She'd also agreed to forego men until she became serious about just one. Now, two months later, she'd already signed a lease, found a job and developed an intense attraction with Kit.

Whereas Mackenzie was undergoing the opposite process. She'd left her long-time career as a buyer in the sweets division of Regal Foods and had invested all her savings in her own business, a penny-candy store called Sweet Something. She'd let go of her steady old boyfriend, Jason Dole, even though being single again after several years of comfortable, if unexciting, companionship made her feel like an untethered kite. Last of all, she'd agreed to put herself in the hands of a stylist and personal shopper and was on the way to a brand-new look, just in time for her store's grand opening.

Cutting her waist-length hair was the last step. One she'd been resisting.

She'd always been comfortable with long hair, simply because she'd always had it. She was a person who rarely ventured outside her comfort zone.

Yes, that was her reasoning and she was sticking to it. It wasn't as if she was actually hiding behind her hair. And she certainly wasn't still clinging to an ancient memory of Devlin, who'd once said...

Mackenzie closed her eyes, succumbing to a moment of pure longing. All she had was memories, but they were enough to make a hot flush of desire rush up her throat.

Nonsense. Her lids popped open and she stared at the distorted reflection of her pink face in the salon's glass doors.

*Nostalgia,* she thought. *Nothing more.*

It had been nearly ten years since she'd seen her high-school crush, Devlin Brandt. Even so, she'd never forgotten that he'd once complimented her on her hair—which had been about the nicest thing he'd ever said to her. Far better than the "Thanks, cutie," or "What would I do without you, Mack?" comments he'd usually tossed her. Like fish from a seal trainer.

By God! She wasn't balancing *that* ball on her nose for another instant.

Mackenzie tucked her bag under her arm and whipped the braid over her shoulder. "Let's go."

Sabrina groaned. "We can't leave. I bargained my soul for this appointment after you broke the first one. Costas is booked months in advance—"

Mackenzie interrupted. "No, let's go *inside*." It was

true that she'd already backed out once. She would not do that again, even though her heart was going *thumpety-thump.* "I'm ready to make good on our bet."

"Oh. Well, that's great." Sabrina's enthusiasm was obviously dimming now that it appeared Mackenzie would follow through. Despite Sabrina's easy-come, easy-go attitude, she didn't want to lose the ring they'd both treasured since they were little girls. That meant she'd have to stick with her promise to keep out of Kit's bed...even if the only way to cure her sexual cravings was to gorge on enough chocolate to dip the Statue of Liberty.

Mackenzie's thoughts returned to her own most wicked temptation. As always, she got no satisfaction. Devlin was merely a fantasy, not a flesh-and-blood, here-and-now partner like Sabrina's Kit.

While Sabrina had once known about her younger sister's crush on the high-school bad boy, it was far too embarrassing for Mackenzie to admit that she still thought of him a decade later.

Every now and then.

Like whenever she brushed her hair.

In a moment of unusual whimsy, Devlin had said that her long dark hair made her look like an evil sorceress—the opposite of the fair-haired, smiley-faced princesses who ruled their school. Mackenzie, forever a "good girl," wasn't even close to being bad, so naturally she'd loved the comparison.

The problem was that Devlin had shown no sign of being bewitched himself.

And now Mackenzie was grown-up. Devlin was a distant memory. She had to give him up, forever, for good.

Sabrina was holding the salon door open. Mackenzie sucked up her courage and sailed on through it. Time for her to *cut* that man right out of her hair!

# 1

*Two weeks later*

"I WAS CRAZY to think that Devlin would be at the reunion," Mackenzie Bliss said, working her tailbone even farther into the padded seat.

She received only a grunt in response, but that didn't faze her.

"Y'know, it's bad enough that it's raining and my new shoes hurt and the spiked punch has given me a headache," she grumbled, pouring out all her complaints. She was in her safety zone, the one place where she could make an anonymous confession. "What's worse is that my stylist persuaded me to wear a panty shaper. Do you know what a panty shaper is? No? I'll tell you. It's a girdle in disguise, that's what it is." She tugged up the tail of her blouse and poked a finger into the bulge rising from her tight waistband. "See that? Like a lump of dough overflowing the pan."

Before her confessor could look—should he even want to—she let the blouse fall across her slumped midriff. "But the worst, the absolute

worst, is that I wasted four hours of my brand-
new life and four hours of the brand-new fabulous me waiting for a man who was *never* going
to show. I'm deluded, is what I am. Deluded!''
She tossed up her hands.

They fell limply onto the seat. She didn't have
the energy to work up a really good snit. The disappointment of missing Devlin was too heavy,
despite all her resolutions that she was never going to think of him again. She hadn't realized until tonight what a large part of her motivation for
change had come from the ever-so-slight possibility of seeing him again at the reunion of their
high-school graduating class.

''It was my tenth high-school reunion, did I tell
you that?''

''Uh-huh.''

''Of course Devlin wouldn't come. He was the
baddest of the high-school bad boys. By the very
definition of bad boy, he wouldn't come. Re-
unions are for ex-cheerleaders and the jocks who
haven't lost their hair yet. The geek who made a
mil with a dot com, maybe. Girls who organized
the car washes and decorated for school dances?
Def'nitely.''

*That's me*, she thought. *You can cut my hair and
dress me up, you can give me a trendy business and a
feature article in* The Village Voice, *but I'm still the
girl who did Devlin's homework.*

*Not the one he kissed.*

"Poor, poor, pitiful me," she muttered.

The cab screeched to a stop near her building on West 17th in Chelsea, a gently aged brownstone with rent control. She paid the driver—who hadn't spoken a word the entire trip—and shoveled herself out of the back seat, gathering her belongings with an unusual carelessness. When the booklet from the reunion fell into the puddle at the curb, she left it, feeling too disconsolate to make the effort. The thing was useless anyway. Although many of her classmates had provided lists of degrees, childrens' ages, home and e-mail addresses, for Devlin there was nothing. Only an old senior photo and a name.

*Devlin Brandt.*

Halfway through the evening, she'd taken one of the keepsake pens off a crepe-ribboned table and scrawled *MIA?* beside his name. At the tail end of the party, having finally worked up some punch-drunk courage, she'd gone around asking about him.

The majority hadn't seen Devlin since graduation day, when he'd arrived halfway through the ceremony on a dinged-up Indian motorcycle and then taken off with a diploma tucked in the front of his jacket and Misty "Most likely to become a Hooters girl" Michaelson whooping it up behind him.

Those who knew Devlin, or had heard rumors of him, had two words for Mackenzie: *Stay away*.

He was into bad stuff, they said. She asked what "bad stuff" meant and got back vague mutterings about shady characters, criminal operations and stolen goods. He'd spent at least a year in prison for burglary, someone claimed, one guy whose car dealership had gone under, admitted that he'd run into Devlin at a Yonkers pawnshop where the owner was known for being less than scrupulous about the goods he handled. Apparently the Rolex watches and diamond dinner rings collected from suburbanites who'd missed a payment on their SUVs were just for show. The real action took place under the counter. And Devlin was in on it.

Or maybe not. No one seemed to know for sure.

Mackenzie had finally tracked down Louie Scheck, who'd lived next door to Devlin's parents. Louie said that his mom said that Mr. and Mrs. Brandt had washed their hands of Devlin after years of trouble had culminated in a prison sentence. He was rotten, plain and simple. Being a nice girl, Mackenzie would stay away if she knew what was good for her.

*Stay away.*

Wise advice, she supposed, but there was no need for it. She'd never even had the chance to get close.

Mackenzie jumped up onto the sidewalk as the cab drove away, spraying dirty rainwater on her shoes and hose. She tilted her head back, meaning to let out a deep sigh. A short huff was all she managed. Between the panty shaper and her underwire bra, she hadn't taken a deep breath all night. You were really in sorry shape when you couldn't even sigh.

The rain increased, pattering her face and running cold down the back of her exposed neck. A streak of mascara came off on the back of her hand when she swiped at her eyes.

Right. The perfect end to a perfect evening.

She trudged up the stoop, sliding her keys from the skimpy evening purse which was on a chain, slung over her shoulder. Raindrops dripped from the ivy that grew in a thick ruff over the lintel. The slap of footsteps running up the street made her turn, but before she could blink the blurry wetness from her eyes she was slammed from behind by a large, wet male. *Whump.* He had her up against the door.

Terror ripped through Mackenzie. She opened her mouth to scream, and the assailant clamped a hand over the lower half of her face. She bit at his palm, squirming against the pressure of his body plastered to hers.

*Instep.* She stomped.

*Rib cage.* She elbowed.

*Scream!* Filled with frantic strength, she wrenched her face away, gulped air and let out a howl that was immediately cut off when he slapped his hand over her mouth again.

"I'm not here to hurt you." He panted heavily in her ear. "Promise."

As if she believed that. Her idea of "hurt" and his were miles apart.

She went against instinct and forced herself to stop struggling, as though she were mollified by his words. She was thinking *groin shot,* if only she could get a leg free. The painful high heels she'd been dying to take off might yet turn out to be a smart purchase.

"Put the key in the door. We're going inside."

She made a muffled sound of protest against his hand. He didn't wait for her to comply, just pried the keys out of her fingers and tried each one in the lock until he found the key that opened the vestibule door.

Her mind raced. Defense class had taught her to never let an attacker get you alone. There was no way she was going into her apartment with a stranger.

He muttered something that ended in "Hurry," and shoved open the door, propelling her inside. His arms were around her waist like iron bars. She slumped, making herself awkward and heavy in hope that his grip would loosen and she could get away. One of her neighbors would hear if she let out a good, hearty scream.

The plan didn't work. He jammed his thigh between her legs and boosted her body across the small lobby. The shock of the contact froze her reactions for an instant. Three steps and they were at the door. Her jagged thoughts splintered. It was just her luck to be in 1A. *But how had he known that?*

Mackenzie renewed her fight when he moved his arm to thrust her key into the lock. She got one hand free and blindly reached back to rake her nails across his face. *Eyeball gouge.*

"Damn, that hurt," he growled, shoving his face tight up against the side of her head. She flailed. "Stop it. *I won't hurt you.*"

His breath was hot on her face. His mouth—

The feel of his mouth moving against her cheek was horrifying. Again, her attempt at a scream was smothered by his hand. She bucked violently, trying to throw them both off their feet. All that did was send her headfirst into the door. It banged open and suddenly they were inside.

He let her go. A panicked cry tore from her throat. *"Help!"*

The door slammed, cutting off her best chance to alert a neighbor. Instead, she plunged into her dark front hallway.

His voice, roughened but soft, came from behind her. "Mackenzie, please..."

*He knew her name!* Somehow, that was worse. The attack was personal now.

She bolted.

The living room was on the right, but she ran past it, not wanting to be cornered in a room without an exit. The bed and bathroom were at the end of the hall. The bath was closer but she veered at the last instant into her bedroom, where there was a phone. And a window and door onto the enclosed courtyard.

She tried to slam the bedroom door behind her, but he was already standing in the jamb, holding it open. She had a fleeting glimpse of a battered face before she whirled away. Her eyes went first to the back door—locked. Was she desperate enough to throw herself through the window? It was too dark to see much, but suddenly she was confused. As if…

"Mackenzie. I'm sorry. I didn't mean to scare you."

*Sorry?* The familiarity in his voice was eerie, but she wasn't about to confront him. Shuddering, she rushed to the window. He must be insane. A stalker.

The window stuck, the wooden sashes swollen by the damp weather. She was gasping, pushing futilely at the double-hung window, when the intruder's hand closed over her shoulder.

In a last-ditch effort, she dove onto the bed, stretching for the phone on the nightstand. He crawled on top of her, dragging her hands away. "No," she sobbed. "Don't—"

"Mackenzie, it's me."

The calmness of his hushed voice reached her. She stopped struggling. "Wh-who?"

He let up a little, and she was able to turn her head. Lightning flashed, illuminating the room for an instant. She saw his face for the first time. It was dreadfully familiar.

"D-Devlin?" She sucked in a shuddery gasp, unable to catch her breath. Her mind spun with disbelief. "Devlin Brandt?"

He eased his hold on her, but didn't let go entirely. They lay flat on the bed, him on top of her twisted body, with his hands cuffing her wrists on either side of her head. Face-to-face.

The moment was surreal. No more than fifteen minutes ago, she had been staring at his senior-class photo in the reunion booklet. Longing for him. That Devlin was a brash kid with a wise-ass grin and long-lashed green eyes, whose silky brown hair had a chestnut sheen.

This man was not the same, even if she discounted the scrapes and swelling of his beat-up face. His eyes were hardened, maybe mean. His hair was dark and stringy. There were hollows in his cheeks, stubble on his jaw, a thin scar above his lip. But he was Devlin. Her vision blurred. One image superimposed over the other. She shut her eyes. Opened them again.

*Devlin Brandt*. Unbelievable! "What the—"

"I'm sorry," he said at the same time.

"You're *sorry*?" She grappled with him, yanking her wrists from his grasp, but he wouldn't release her even when she boxed his ear. "Let…me…go!"

"Promise you won't call 9-1-1."

"Why shouldn't I?" Her voice escalated. "You grab me at my door, *force* me inside—"

"I was in a hurry. There wasn't time to stand around and chitchat."

"You scared me!"

"There was no other choice. I had to make a fast move."

She was remembering how she'd been warned away from him. He's dangerous to know, her classmates had said. Involved in criminal activity. By the looks of him, he wasn't even successful at it. There was a scrape on his jaw and a lump on his forehead. One eye was swelling shut.

She panted, growing aware of the dampness of their clothing and the compromising position in which he had her. Devlin was heavy on top of her. The smell of his soaked leather jacket was strong, and his hair was dripping wet. He'd been out in the rain for a while. Lurking? Then why had he overtaken her? Why didn't he let her go? None of this made sense.

Various observations that had been pushed aside in her fear came floating to the forefront. He'd known who she was when he grabbed her.

He'd even known which apartment was hers. His motive was obviously crooked....

"What's going on?" she demanded. "How did you find me?"

"The reunion."

"What does that mean?"

"I saw your name and address in the list they sent out with the invitations."

*Right.* "But there wasn't any contact information for *you*," she pointed out, "so how did you receive the list in the first place?" Part of her recognized that it was absurd to debate details when her teenage crush turned ex-con was holding her tight in the missionary position of her schoolgirl dreams. How many times had she wished to have Devlin Brandt look at her as closely as he was right now?

A self-conscious warmth crept over her. She was no more a pretty sight than he. Her makeup was smeared, her shorn hair was plastered to her head, her carefully chosen outfit was a total mess—

And she was wearing a stretchy pink Lycra panty girdle.

*Oh, hell.*

"I have my ways," Devlin said.

She narrowed her eyes. "Criminal ways."

His face hovered over hers in the dark. Close enough for her to see that despite his condition, his grin was as impudent as ever. "You've followed my career."

"Hardly. But I got an earful at the reunion."

"Was that tonight?" He angled his head, looking down at her cleavage, which the underwire bra had pushed into the unbuttoned vee of her blouse and halfway toward her chin. The pearl necklace was tossed to one side, following the curve of her breast. "Is that why you're all dressed up?"

Exasperating. She rolled her eyes upward and stared at the ceiling through wet, clumpy lashes. "Are you ever going to let me up?"

The timbre of his voice dropped an octave. A helluva sexy octave. "I'm considering it."

"Decide fast," she said through her teeth. "Before I start screaming again." Now that her terror was gone—most of it, anyway—the sheer bulk of him was starting to affect her. He was heavy, hard and thoroughly muscled. She still couldn't draw an even breath. Every time she tried, her breasts swelled, the tips rubbing against the open zipper of his leather jacket. If he didn't let go soon, any screaming she did was going to be in ecstasy.

Thunder rumbled. "You've done enough of that," he said, and she hoped he wasn't able to read her thoughts. "I'll be lucky if you didn't alert the entire block."

"What did you expect? Have you never heard of walking up to a person and saying hello?"

His eyes glowed an otherworldly green in the sudden flash of lightning. "I told you—there wasn't time."

She turned her head aside, unable to reason under his blatant scrutiny. "I don't understand."

"Mackenzie…" He sounded regretful. "I wouldn't be here if I'd had any other choice." He lifted his head, listening. Soft, surreptitious sounds came from outside.

He released her arms and stealthily levered himself off her, pausing to stroke two fingertips over her mouth. "Shh."

There was a metallic clatter. Sounded like a garbage can lid to Mackenzie. Cats, she thought. Or rats.

Devlin was holding himself very still above her. She compressed her tingling lips, waiting. Rain pelted the windowpane. A truck drove by on the street out front, its engine grinding. Her heartbeat hammered. Distant honking and gleeful shouts from the neighborhood's night people brought the outside world into their tense little cocoon.

She rose to her elbows. "Don't move," Devlin whispered. He stood and crossed to the window, as silent and skulking as a cat. The shade was up, the drapes open. He slithered to one side and peered outside, then slowly drew the curtains shut.

"See anything?" she asked when he remained by the window, watching from the side. Finally he reached past the curtains and closed the blind with a snap.

"No." But his face was drawn into a worried frown.

She sat up on the edge of the bed and rearranged her rumpled clothing. One of her shoes had come off in the chase. Two buttons had popped off her silk blouse and the sleeves of the short fitted jacket that matched her skirt had been torn at the seams. Her blouse hung loose, concealing her bulging waist, so she pulled off the jacket and folded it meticulously before she set it aside.

She looked up and saw Devlin watching her, his head cocked. "I'm nervous," she said, feeling defensive. Anxiety tended to turn her into a fussbudget. After the divorce, her teenage bedrooms had always been surgically neat.

He shrugged. "Listen, I know this seems crazy, but you have to trust me—"

A loud *bzzzz* silenced him. The intercom buzzer at her front door had gone off.

Devlin cursed a single epithet.

She winced at the harsh word. Not that she didn't hear it every day out on the street a thousand times over—just never in her bedroom.

And how telling was that? she wondered. Her sex life was drab and unexciting, exactly like her last relationship. But *now* was not the time to worry over it!

"Don't answer that," Devlin said when the buzzer rang again in a loud, annoying *blat.*

After a couple of seconds, she heard the faint buzz at her neighbor's door. Her bedroom shared a wall with Blair Boback's living room. "They're trying all the apartments."

"Damn." Devlin grabbed Mackenzie's arm and towed her to the front door, heedless that she'd lost a shoe and was staggering crookedly. He stepped over her upended purse and listened at the door, then looked through the peephole. Abruptly, he drew back. Though he didn't change expression or tense up, she sensed the freeze in him.

The lobby door clanged open and shut. "One of the other tenants buzzed them through," she guessed. A large part of her was frightened more by Devlin than the interlopers who'd just gained access to the building. *They* could be harmless. Devlin was…not.

He squinted at her, his left eye practically swollen shut. A blue shadow ringed it. "Them?"

"Them. Him. Her." She tried to act defiant. "It could be the entire roster of the New York Jets, for all I know."

Her doorbell ding-donged. She jumped. He

tightened his fingers, digging them into the fleshy part of her arm as he put his mouth to her ear. "Don't answer."

"But…"

*Bam, bam, bam.* They were pounding at her door, so forcefully the hinges rattled.

She shoved her damp bangs off her face with the back of one wrist. "Let me look," she whispered.

Devlin shook his head.

"Is someone after you?"

"Shh. I'm listening."

The uninvited visitors had moved to the next apartment. Mackenzie pressed her ear to the door. Low rumbles interspersed with a higher-pitched, and increasingly excited, response. "My neighbor," she said, so worried she had to resist smoothing wrinkles from Devlin's creased leather jacket. Her fingers itched to smooth his hair. "Blair Boback."

Devlin's face was grim. "I hope she's smart enough not to let them into her apartment."

Mackenzie smiled mirthlessly. "Oh, yeah. Blair's street savvy."

They heard Blair's door close. Devlin watched through the peephole. "Going upstairs," he said. "How many apartments in this building?"

"Only eight."

He released a breath and leaned against the wall—big, dark, wet and punk-tough against her peach-and-cream-striped damask. "When they don't find me upstairs, they're going to come back to your door." Again, Devlin swore. "They must have seen which building I went into."

"They?"

He didn't answer.

"*They* might be canvassing the entire street."

"Maybe." He paused. "Here's what I want you to do. Open the door, chain on, when they come back. They ask about me, you say you know nothing and shut the door. Be convincing." He gave her the hard look again, his fingers squeezing her arm like barbecue tongs. "*Very* convincing."

She spoke tentatively. "What if I don't want to—"

He was fast. Before she could blink, he was standing directly in front of her, both hands on her now, dragging her close against his chest. He glared, their faces inches apart. His jaw was clenched, his nostrils flared. It wouldn't be a shock if he snorted and pawed the ground like a bull. The move was supposed to be intimidating—and it was—but the greater threat was the way he made her feel.

*Alive.* Scared, but so incredibly alive. Her heart was pounding, her blood racing. She was sharply aware of every pleasure point on her body. The distant yearning she was so familiar with had become a strange and potent hunger....

"You'll do it," Devlin said grittily.

"Or what?" *He's a criminal,* she reminded herself. *Not the cool high-school bad boy you remember.* The potential for trouble that she'd once found so fascinating had been fulfilled. And there was nothing alluring about knowing that he'd committed actual crimes.

Devlin's lips came down on hers, knocking out every objection with one striking blow. He didn't kiss—he attacked. His mouth was hot and his tongue was wicked, thrusting against hers with no pretense at pretty seduction. His teeth ground against her lower lip as he bit and sucked and drove his tongue deeper. The shock was staggering. She hadn't known that a kiss could be so unapologetically savage and still turn her molten with desire.

This couldn't be happening! *Oh God, oh please, oh please don't—*

Devlin wrenched his mouth away. His slitted eyes glittered with what seemed like a mocking, devilish intent.

Mackenzie was paralyzed, swaying on her frozen feet. When she licked her lips, she tasted a drop of blood.

"Or what?" was all she could think to say in a hoarse, thready voice.

"Or I'll never kiss you like that again."

Her eyes widened.

"Dammit, Mackenzie." Devlin was obviously frustrated with her. He gave her shoulders a small, hard shake. "Do what I say. If you don't, there'll be violence. Your nice clean walls will get all messed up. I hear blood is hell to get out of silk."

He didn't have to shake her; she was already

trembling. "You wouldn't hurt me," she blurted, but she didn't sound so positive, even to herself. Especially to herself. Her lips were so raw it hurt to speak.

"It won't be you," he said. "It'll be me."

She blinked. Did he mean that he'd be the one who got hurt? Or that he'd be spilling a third party's blood? "I don't understand—"

Devlin released her with a rough shove. Her teeth came together with a click as she stumbled, then regained her balance. He'd turned his back to her and was looking through the peephole again. "You'll get me killed," he said.

Too much to absorb. She rubbed at the goose bumps on her arms, then lifted her foot and pulled off the remaining shoe. Part of her wanted to run, even though there was nowhere to go. She held the designer pump in her hand, weighing it as a weapon. The spiked heel could be lethal.

Devlin whirled around. "They're coming back. Get ready."

Panic hit her. She dropped the shoe and rubbed at her face as if she could erase his kiss. Her hair was a mess, and her blouse— She looked down. Half undone. Her peach lace La Perla bra showed in the gap between buttons.

The bell rang. She didn't move except to clutch at the front of her blouse. Devlin had to push her resisting body toward the door. "Tell them you were sleeping. And whatever you do, don't look at me."

With a trembling hand, she reached for the doorknob. "Who is it?" she warbled.

"Police."

She flinched in surprise. Police? Devlin wanted her to lie to the *police?*

She glanced at him, standing close beside her. His expression was black, ungiving. His hand had closed on the back of her neck and she had the feeling that he could easily pick her up and give her a shake. It was pretty clear, even in her frazzled state—he was the alpha wolf and she was a whimpering puppy, showing her belly in surrender.

*Be brave.* She cleared her throat to strengthen her voice as she put her eye to the door. "Let me see your badges."

Something that might have been a badge flashed past the peephole. In the fisheye lens, she saw two men standing at her doorstep. One was older and squatter than the other, but they were both wet and disgruntled, dressed in limp, wrinkled suits and ties. They could be cops. But then they also could be rent collectors, insurance salesmen or…hit men.

"Open up," the older one barked. He had a gun, she saw, holstered beneath his unbuttoned jacket. He reached across his chest and put his hand on it. Not an insurance salesman, then.

Mackenzie looked at Devlin. He returned the stare, his face drawn tight and pale. Once she opened the door, it would be just as easy for her to turn him in, and he must know it. Maybe there'd be a tussle, but if he surrendered with his hands up, no bloodshed would be involved.

Probably not. Chances were slim. But was she willing to gamble that Devlin would surrender without a fight?

The cops hammered at her door. "What do you want?" she asked.

"We're looking for a man. He's armed and dangerous."

Devlin's fingers clamped on her nape. Not hurtfully, but another shock ran through her. Her instincts were confused, fizzing and snapping in every direction like Pop Rocks. She didn't know what to do.

"All right," she said, turning the locks. Obviously she hadn't locked them when she'd "arrived" home—at the time, she'd been frightened for her life. That meant Devlin had done it. Before he'd come after her. Whether or not he was armed and dangerous, he was certainly cool and calculating.

*And hot and primal.*

She took a deep breath and opened the door a couple of inches. The two men pressed closer, their faces leering. The older one reached for his gun. She let out a squeak and slammed the door shut.

They pounded on it, shouting at her. "Lady— open up!"

"Put the gun away first," she demanded. "I don't believe in guns."

Out of the corner of her eye, she saw Devlin crack a small smile.

The cops made complaining noises, but they conceded, stepping back from her door with their hands hanging at their sides. She stared through the peephole for several seconds, then reopened the door. "What's this about?"

The older one spoke. He had a deep voice, a craggy face and a big gold watch on his wrist. "A violent criminal is on the loose in the neighborhood. Have you been home all evening, ma'am? Have you seen or heard anything suspicious?"

"I—" She pressed her tender lips together, wincing at the pain. Devlin crowded her, guarding the door, but keeping just out of sight. "I was sleeping."

The cop ran his eyes over the narrow slice of her that was visible through the gap in the door. "In your clothes?"

She gave a shamefaced shrug. "It was a long day, Officer…?" She squinted. "Can I see those badges again?"

"So you haven't seen a man? About six foot, brown hair, leather jacket and, uh, black jeans? He's got a scar, here—" The gray-haired cop drew a finger above his upper lip and something in his eyes made her wary of him. The gesture seemed gloating, even depraved. She struggled not to glance at Devlin for reassurance.

*Reassurance?* Well. That settled it. She hesitated for only a second before answering. "No. Absolutely not. I haven't seen him."

"Can we come in and look?" the second guy said. He smiled. He was handsome, but the smile was oiled, as if he practiced it so frequently it slid across his face with no effort or sincerity. "A woman like you, alone in a ground-floor apartment..." He tried to peer past her into the hallway. The smile flickered, then went out. "Could be dangerous."

"I'm fine," she said. "Completely alone. But thank you for the concern."

"All right, ma'am," said the other one. "You be sure to keep a lookout."

"I'll call the local precinct if I see him," she said. "This, uh, criminal you're after."

A worried expression passed over the face of the taller cop.

The other simply nodded. "We'll be in the neighborhood for a while, if you need us." He swung around to leave, then turned back, drawing a filmy square from his pants pocket. "By the way, is this yours?"

She looked at her scarf. "Why, yes. Where did you find it?"

"Here in the lobby. By the door."

"I must have dropped it on my way home from work," she said.

"It's damp."

She reached a hand through the crack in the door. "Yes. The rain, you know. I'm surprised one of my neighbors didn't pick it up."

He gave her the scarf. His face was closed, but suspicious, she believed. "Be careful, ma'am.

You're a nice lady, I can see." He glowered. "You don't want any trouble."

Her pulse stuttered. Was it a warning? A threat?

Devlin pressed against her so close she swore she could feel his heartbeat. She narrowed the door another inch.

"I will be careful, thank you, Officer. I hope you catch the, um—" She stopped, swallowing nervously. "What's he done, anyway?"

"Just about everything," the older cop said, looking at her with lidded eyes that were as flat and expressionless as a lizard's. "Murder, theft, assault...you name it. The guy we're after is no lightweight criminal. He's an ex-con. Rotten to the core. You don't want anything to do with him."

# 2

DEVLIN EXPECTED Mackenzie to scream, fight, run. Instead she calmly said goodbye to the "officer," then closed and secured the door, turning locks and sliding bolts with a certain steady resolution. *Snick, chunk, chunk.*

She turned to face him. Her eyes were huge and glistening. Her lips were puffy, deepened in color to the bright pink of arousal. She kept touching the raw red spot at the corner of her mouth with her tongue.

Guilt over hurting her threaded through him, but he ignored it. She was a big girl. She could take it.

Her expression had become mulish. She was finally getting ticked by his high-handedness. "All right, now, Devlin. No more lies. I want to know why you kissed me."

*What?* He almost laughed. *That* was what she asked? "Not who I killed?"

"Did you? Kill someone?"

"No."

"And the other charges?"

He dropped his chin a notch, ran a hand through his wet hair. His entire body ached, but he was trying to seem unworried, as if he had no concerns over trusting her with his life when he was beginning to realize that Mackenzie Bliss had changed. She wasn't as reliable as she used to be. Nor as meek.

"Guilty," he said.

She sucked in a gasp. "You've been in prison."

"Yes."

"And you're in trouble again."

"Yes."

"And you—" her tongue flicked over her lip "—you came to me."

"Only because I knew you lived in this area." *And I was running for my life.*

"So I'm a convenience."

"One night," he said. "That's all I need."

"What happens in the morning?"

"Not your concern."

"Argh." Making an irritated sound at his stonewalling, she closed her eyes and rested her head against the door. He wanted to stay there and keep looking at her—keep an eye on her, that was—but Sloss and Bonaventure might still be lurking outside. If he was lucky, they hadn't seen which building he'd entered and were going door-to-door up and down the entire block, as Mackenzie had suggested.

Devlin went into the living room and checked out the front window, parting the moss-colored velvet drapes the smallest sliver. Sloss and Bonny were standing on the street, arguing. Sloss would win, but Bonny wouldn't know it until tomorrow. He was more concerned with dabbing at the watermarks on his hundred-dollar silk tie.

Sloss took out a cell phone and had a brief conversation. Devlin knew what the command from their greedy boss, Boris Cheney aka Fat Man, would be: get the ruby back from Devlin by any means necessary. Sloss was the man for the job. Even the most drastic method wouldn't cost him a wink of sleep, though he didn't look happy about the long night ahead as he flipped up his phone. He and Bonny waited for a delivery van to go by, spraying rainwater from its wheels, before stepping off the curb. Sloss stopped to fish something out of the gutter, but Devlin couldn't see what had interested him. Bonny had already sprinted across the street and was buzzing apartments on the other side, trying to get into another building. That was good. They hadn't pinpointed his location.

Devlin watched until they disappeared inside. There was always some idiot occupant who'd let a stranger in just to stop the buzzer noise from disturbing their TV program.

He turned. Mackenzie was there, waiting, curled up in a big, plush armchair. She'd wrapped her arms around herself to contain her shivering. Cursing the unexpected tenderness she made him feel even now, he took a blanket off the back of the couch and draped it over her.

The room was filled with shadows, but his eyes were accustomed to the dark and he was able to examine her furnishings. Matching decor, flower arrangements, family photos in silver frames. It was exactly the kind of place he'd expected Mackenzie to live in—aside from the lack of smiling hubby and two cherubic children.

He squinted at her. "Thanks for not turning on the lights."

She shrugged.

He sat. No use waiting for an invitation anymore.

Mackenzie was silent. Although she'd calmed down as he'd known she would, she still didn't look particularly accepting of his story. Smart girl.

She put a hand to her hair, restlessly fingering the short strands. He couldn't get used to Mackenzie Bliss with short hair. She'd always had a long, luxuriant mane, the color of sable. Sometimes, back in high school, he'd caught himself wondering how her hair would feel, brushing over his bare chest. And how Mackenzie would feel naked, so soft and warm and curvy no pillows would be necessary if they spent the night together.

She opened her mouth. "I still want to know why you kissed me."

"It was an impulse."

Her eyes glinted like steel. That was new. "No, it wasn't. You had a purpose."

"You're right." She was much sharper than the dreamy girl he remembered. "I needed to convince you."

"And you thought kissing me was the way to do

it?'' She tried to sound insulted, but the quaver in her voice betrayed her. "Do I look that des—that stupid?"

"Not stupid," he said. *And not desperate, either.*

"Then what?" she snapped.

He gave her a cocky, I-know-you-think-I'm-sexy grin. "Susceptible."

She clamped her lips shut and let a silence well between them, a silence filled with their mutual knowledge that she'd had a crush on him all through high school and that he'd known it and used her devotion to his advantage whenever it suited him. He hadn't been cruel or thoughtless with her feelings. But he had taken her for granted, letting her do the homework he'd neglected, relying on her cram sessions to get him through exams, allowing her to cover for him when there'd been a school vandalism investigation. Back then, the one constant in his life was that she'd always been there, ready and eager to help, gazing adoringly up at him through her big dark eyes. She'd made him feel valuable, important. The buddies who'd believed they were so tough had mocked her as Little Miss Priss and urged Devlin to get into her pants already, but he'd actually liked and respected Mackenzie. She was a nice girl. He'd kept his hands off her because he knew she "loved" him and there was no way he was getting involved in heavy shit like that.

A good plan, even now. No doubt her crush was long over, but he was betting that she had remained the type of girl who took sex and relationships seriously. He never had and never could, as long as he continued in his present circumstances.

"Susceptible," she repeated scornfully. "You have got to be kidding. High school was ten years ago. I'm not the innocent, gullible schoolgirl I was then."

But she *had* covered for him. He wondered why.

Not because of the kiss. It had been even more fierce than he'd intended. Once he'd felt her mouth under his, sensation had taken over. Yes, his intentions had been manipulative and crude. But the emotion that had resulted was unexpected.

Blame it on auld lang syne. High-school reunion. Lost youth. *A handy excuse,* said the distant, stubborn, ethical part of him that refused to die.

"So then why don't you call the cops," he said, getting an idea.

Her head jerked up. "What?"

"Tell them there are two suspicious men prowling the area. You don't have to leave your name."

"But..." She blinked a couple of times, scowling deeply as the various scenarios hit home. He could tell when she figured it out. She inhaled with amazement, her mouth dropping open. "Those men aren't the police."

He ticked a finger at her.

"Who are they?"

Sloss and Bonny were in charge of a ring of thieves and petty criminals who fenced their goods at Cheney's pawnshops. Devlin was supposedly one of their minions. For now Mackenzie would have to believe that.

"You don't want to know." He cut her off when she started to protest. "Trust me, the less I tell you, the better."

"God, Devlin. What are you involved in?"

He shifted, becoming more and more aware of that uneasy, niggling voice inside him. Enough common decency was buried somewhere in there that he knew he shouldn't be using Mackenzie this way. His being in her neighborhood wasn't as complete a coincidence as he wanted her to believe. Ever since he'd seen the reunion invitation and class roster a month ago, he'd been thinking about her. Curiosity, he'd told himself, and nothing more. No way was he planning to come near her—that was too dangerous for both of them.

Yet here he was.

The irony was not delicious.

"I know, I know," she said. "If you tell me, you have to kill me." She laughed with a hollow sarcasm.

"That's not even funny."

Her face fell. She nipped at her bottom lip, then winced when that hurt. "Why do you want me to call the cops? I would think you wouldn't want them anywhere near here."

"They'll do at least a drive-by and Sloss—" He tilted his head toward the street. "Those two will leave. Then *I* can leave." He paused. "That's what you want, right?"

"Yes, of course. But I don't want you to get killed, either."

"I'll go out the back."

"There's not much cover back there. What if they're waiting for you?"

Devlin had thought of that. Sloss was a bulldog—slow, thorough and unrelenting. He'd nose into every building and sniff out every avenue of escape before he was satisfied that Devlin had given them the slip. Even police intervention wouldn't keep Sloss out of the way for long.

"Are you arguing for me to stay?"

Mackenzie looped the blanket over her shoulders, shawl-style. Her hair had dried into spikes and her nylons bagged at her knees and ankles. She looked like a punk grandma. "I guess you can sleep on the couch."

"Thanks." He let out a soft groan as he settled back. His ribs ached fiercely from Bonaventure's vicious kicks. Judging by the stickiness where his shirt was plastered to his skin, the nasty thug had managed to draw blood, as well. After Bonny had caught Devlin supposedly stealing from the latest haul, he'd called in Sloss and they'd taken him to a waterfront warehouse and alternated between questioning and beating him. He hadn't given up a single incriminating detail. After three months on this job, there was no way in hell he'd be made by two small-time crooks.

Mackenzie sat forward, rocking nervously. "Okay. I'll make the call, if you think that will scare them off.

But first you have to tell me the truth. How did you land on my doorstep? Were you waiting for me to come home?"

"No. This isn't a social call, Mackenzie. I swear I wouldn't be here if those two thugs hadn't been breathing down my neck. I never meant to endanger you."

"Yet you were 'in the neighborhood.' You knew my address."

"I explained that. It was coincidence." A slight exaggeration. He'd thought he'd lost Sloss and Bonny the first time, after he'd worked free of the ropes and slipped out of the warehouse while they argued over what to do with him. Getting out of their neighborhood had seemed like a good idea—until he realized that he had no money, no weapon, no ID and nowhere to go. It wasn't as though he could walk into a pawn shop and cash out the ruby he'd managed to squirrel away.

He'd headed for Broadway, where there would be plenty of people around for safety. Because Mackenzie had been on his mind—he had to think of something pleasant and real to keep himself from crossing the line into the dark side—he'd thought of crashing with her as a last resort, but only if it had been a one-hundred-percent safe situation. By a twist of perverse luck, Sloss and Bonny had spotted him on Broadway, heading this way. Desperation had brought him running to Mackenzie's door, minutes ahead of the pair of henchmen.

Devlin would have rather kept on going, but when he saw her on the street and knew she'd recognize him there was no other option.

If lady luck was shining on him, Sloss and Bonny had believed her when she'd spoken to them at the door and wouldn't be back.

If not...Mackenzie would need watching. Now that he'd dragged her into this, he'd have to protect her. A complication he didn't need, even though she sure was a sight for sore eyes. And a deadened heart.

She grimaced, still not trusting him. "You should have come to the reunion instead, and spared yourself the...whatever it is you're up to."

"I'm not one of our old high school's shining success stories."

"Yeah, well, maybe you should reconsider your career path, huh?"

He wasn't going to follow that line of discussion. "Make the call, Mackenzie. Then we can get some sleep."

She stood and moved silently through the living room on unshod feet, picking up a cordless phone from the desk beneath the window. Despite her disheveled state, she was even prettier than he'd remembered. In school, she'd been plump and quiet, something of a wallflower who'd been overshadowed by her active, outgoing sister. The past ten years had been good to her. The baby-fat face had gained more definition, and the womanly figure now suited her.

Suited him, too. The feel of her breasts pushing against his chest had been quite the distraction.

Thoughtfully, she touched the phone to her chin as she walked back across the room. "Let me get this straight. You memorized *my* address from the sheet sent out with the invitation to the reunion. Then you just *happened* to be on this particular street, needing a hideout...at the *very* moment that I was coming home from our tenth high-school reunion. And *then*, instead of saying hello and introducing yourself properly, you attacked me and pushed me inside because you were in a—" she made quotation marks in the air "—*hurry*." She plopped down beside him on the couch. "Have I got it right?"

"More or less."

She shook her head as she dialed. "Just so you don't think I'm swallowing that baloney."

He grabbed the phone and hit the hang-up button "Don't use 9-1-1. They can trace your call." He punched in a number. "Here, I dialed the precinct direct. But be brief and hang up fast."

She hesitated before taking a breath and speaking in the querulous high-pitched voice of an old lady. "I want to report suspicious activity. West 17th in Chelsea, between Sixth and Seventh. Two men. They're busting into apartment buildings." She cut the connection. "How was that?"

Devlin smiled, thinking of Sloss and Bonny scrambling for cover when the N.Y.P.D. arrived. The interruption wasn't more than a wrench in their plans, but even a minor victory was satisfying after the disastrous evening he'd had. Three month's work was on the verge of collapsing. "You did good."

Her serious expression lightened. "*Shew*. Does this make me a gun moll?"

"Only for the night."

Her cheeks curved with a smile. "This has been one hell of a night."

"Fun reunion?"

"It wasn't all that I'd hoped."

"Why not? Looks like you've done well for yourself."

She adjusted the gap in her blouse, then squared her shoulders and lifted her chin, giving him another glimpse of her new, confident attitude. "Well, yes, as a matter of fact, I have."

"Still working for the candy company?"

She blinked. "How do you know where I worked? We haven't seen each other since high school."

"I keep my ear to the ground. I hear things." He wasn't about to tell her that he'd purposely kept track of her when it hadn't meant anything special. He'd been curious, that's all. "You went to college and started at Regal right after graduation. I bet you're a vice president by now."

"Actually, I've moved on. Just recently. I opened my own penny-candy emporium in the Village a couple of weeks ago. It's called Sweet Something. Several of the city newspapers ran items about the grand opening party. Mostly because my publicist got a few celebrities to come, but even so..."

He grinned, delighted with the wholesome rightness of her fate. By damn, the world hadn't gone all wrong, not if Mackenzie Bliss owned a candy store. "I remember," he said. "You always carried butterscotch candies in your backpack. And—" He searched his memory.

"Sugar Babies," she said. "I had a minor fling with Zowies in eighth grade."

"Still have all your teeth?" he teased.

She displayed them. "A couple of cavities. One root canal."

On impulse, he touched the nick at the corner of her mouth. "Sorry about that."

She pulled away, her lashes lowering as she slid a thumb over her lip. The gesture seemed too girlish for a twenty-eight-year-old woman.

"Do you have a boyfriend?" he asked abruptly.

"I did, but, um, not anymore." She showed her teeth again, going for a feral female look that didn't suit her. Not even the new her. "I dumped him."

"Yeah?"

She frowned. "You don't believe me?"

"Why wouldn't I?"

A heightened blush betrayed her. "Okay. It was more like a mutual breakup. The relationship died from natural causes, although I was the one who finally pointed it out. And it took me only two years to notice." Her face changed. "This is dumb. You're on the run and I'm talking about penny candy and my ex-boyfriend. Give me your jacket. It's so wet it's soaking through the couch.''

"This is the only chance we'll have to catch up," he said to distract her. It was better if he kept the jacket.

"Our one and only chance," she said with an edge. "Right. So, you have my story. My parents got remarried, by the way. Almost three months ago. And my sister—remember her?—has moved to Manhattan. She's working in a Tribeca bistro."

"Sabrina Bliss," he said, shaking his head. She was hot sun to Mackenzie's cool shade. "I thought she'd be surfing in Hawaii or partying on a yacht in the Riviera."

"Check back in another ten years. She might be."

"Got a husband?"

"Not Sabrina. At least, not yet."

"How come you're not married?" he asked.

Mackenzie shrugged. "No one's asked me."

"Not even this guy you just dumped?"

"Well..."

"You turned him down? Why?"

Her gaze darted at his face, but she didn't answer, only shook her head. She put on a smile, asking softly, "What about you?"

He knew he shouldn't toy with her, but he couldn't help it. She'd gotten to him. Not only via his overt reactions to her magnificent breasts and sweet mouth, but in some mysterious, subliminal way, just as she used to in high school. "What about me?" he asked, his voice grating as he turned her innocent question around. "Would you turn me down?"

She caught her breath, taking him too seriously. He had to remember that she was prone to doing that. "I guess my answer depends on your question."

His laugh was harsh in his throat. "I'm not asking you to marry me, that's for sure."

"You're already married?" she guessed, flicking her lashes at him again.

"Are you kidding?"

"Why not? I've read about those jailhouse marriages." She reached over to unzip his jacket.

"I haven't spent my entire adult life in prison," he said out of a senseless need to amend her impression of him. She was *supposed* to think he was a lowlife criminal. And he wasn't supposed to care.

She looked disappointed in him. "How are your parents?"

"Still living in Scarsdale." His father, Ed Brandt, was an uncomplicated medical salesman who stayed on the road even longer than his job required. He was avoiding his wife, Marilyn, who wasn't a bad person, but very difficult to live with on a daily basis. She suffered from manic depression, and her moods kept the Brandt household in a constant funk. Devlin avoided them now, but he kept track via his older sister, who was married and happy, the closest thing to normal the family had produced. Ed was nearing retirement and Marilyn was on a new drug, so Devlin guessed they were doing as well as could be expected.

"How's your mother?" Mackenzie's face showed her concern.

"She's feeling a little better, thanks." Devlin cleared his throat, uncomfortable with the subject. He'd been ashamed by his mom as a kid and had never brought friends back to the house. Word had spread about the crazy lady anyway, making him an outcast early on. In Scarsdale, imperfection wasn't tolerated. "My sister, Deb, looks after her."

"Do you visit?"

"Not if I can help it."

Mackenzie gasped. At first he thought she was reacting to his callous disregard for family, but then he realized where she was looking. Her eyes were round. *"Devlin."*

Damn—she'd seen the blood. He should have been paying attention instead of worrying about her opinion to his cover story. And now she'd managed to tug the jacket halfway off him, revealing the red patch on his torn shirt.

"You're hurt." She reached behind the sofa and clicked on a lamp. Her eyes got even bigger as she goggled. "Is it a gunshot wound?"

"No. It's nothing." He pushed her hands away. "Only a scratch."

"Then let me see..." Within seconds, his shirt was unbuttoned and she was examining his abdomen. It was decorated with bruises and a couple of raw red scrapes that matched the one on his chin. Bonaventure had taken great pleasure in stomping him into the cement floor when the first cursory pat-down hadn't turned up the missing ruby.

Devlin sucked air between his teeth when Mackenzie prodded at his ribs. "Broken?" she asked.

"Not for lack of trying," he said.

"You should see a doctor. What if your lung gets punctured?"

"The ribs are only bruised. I've had cracked ribs before and believe me, it hurt like hell. This only hurts like heck."

"That's hardly an educated diagnosis."

"Them's the breaks."

She shook her head. "Why don't you take off those wet boots and go clean up in the bathroom. There's a first-aid kit in the medicine cabinet. I'll make you something hot to drink and get you an ice pack for that eye. Then I can bandage you up."

He put out a hand, stopping her from rising. "Can I trust you?"

She seemed about to give him the sarcastic retort he deserved, but then her features softened. "You must think so, Devlin, or you wouldn't be here."

She was wrong. He'd been a deep undercover cop for so long that he didn't trust anyone, even himself.

# 3

WITH NOT SO MUCH as a backward glance, Devlin went off to the bathroom, holding his side, his boots leaving wet, muddy tracks on her carpet.

Mackenzie stared at her fists, knotted in her lap, until the door closed. Then she bolted for the bedroom, swooping up her discarded purse and shoes along the way. She closed and locked the door. After only the briefest of thoughts about the phone—who would she call, after all, if not the cops? *Sabrina?*—she reached under her skirt and began wiggling out of the ruined hose and confining panty girdle. Not because she was letting Devlin's hands anywhere near the area. Just because.

*Ah, oxygen!* She took a deep breath and let it out noisily. The hamper was in the bathroom with Devlin, so she kicked the offending garments under the bed. No time to be meticulous.

She couldn't put on pajamas and a robe, but she didn't want to look dressed up, either. Frumpy sweats would certainly scare him off, but she wasn't sure she wanted that. Not yet. Might as well admit it—her interest was aroused regardless of the troubling situation.

Deciding on a sweater and jeans, she rummaged through the chest of drawers, startling herself when she glanced in the mirror above it. Raccoon eyes, puffy lips, hair going in every direction—disaster.

"Staying alive is your first concern," she muttered, pulling on the jeans and sweater. To that end, she checked the tiny paved backyard, saw nothing unusual except an overturned garbage can, then grabbed her cell phone from the purse she'd thrown on the bed. A quick peek out the door ascertained that Devlin—*Omigod, Devlin Brandt was in her bathroom!*—was occupied.

It took Blair four rings to answer. Mackenzie ran a hand over her hair, trying to smooth down the bristles.

"Talk dirty to me," Blair said in a husky voice.

Mackenzie exhaled in relief. Her neighbor often answered the phone that way. "Are you okay?"

"Depends what you mean by okay. If the question means is my neck killing me the answer is yes." Blair had perpetual neck strain from a twenty-pound headdress she wore in a cabaret act. "If it means am I being held at gunpoint by a dangerous criminal, then no. A pity. I could use the excitement."

Mackenzie made a small sound of distress. Her knees gave out and she sat on the edge of the bed.

Blair's voice sharpened. "Mackenzie? *You* okay?"

Half a dozen responses ran through her head, but in the end she only said, "Yeah, sure," because there didn't seem to be any way to explain about Devlin and the cops-that-weren't in the five seconds she had to spare. She'd called only to see if Blair was okay.

"I know the police talked to you, too, Mackenzie. I poked my head out. Say *bananas* if you have a madman holding you at gunpoint to keep you quiet."

"Plantains."

Blair started to laugh, then stopped. "Is that a joke, or a code I'm not getting?"

"It's a long story. I'll explain tomorrow. I have to go and make tea now—"

"Wait a minute! I smell cover-up and it's not my makeup."

"Tomorrow," Mackenzie said.

"Hey, what about the reunion?" Blair shrieked, but Mackenzie pretended not to hear. She shoved the phone into her pants pocket, checked the hallway and scurried to the kitchen.

*Tea.* It wasn't easy to concentrate on normal activities when there was a criminal in the bathroom whose kiss had melted her panty shaper, but she filled the kettle, set it on a burner and took down a box of green tea with shaking hands.

"Who'd you call?" Devlin said from behind her.

She jumped. When she whipped around, he was shirtless and startling and she squeezed the box so tight the flap popped open. Tea bags spilled out across the floor. She dropped to her knees to gather them, her mind working, her stomach churning.

Devlin didn't move.

He must have heard her voice on the phone. There

was no use in denying it. "Not the cops. I called Blair. My next-door neighbor." Mackenzie's voice came out so jerky, she was sure he'd think she was lying. "Just to check. I thought—" She shoved a handful of tea bags into the box. "Just to check."

Devlin's stockinged feet moved toward her. She kept her head down. He'd taken off his boots, but his jeans were wet to the knees, black against the faded charcoal where the fabric was especially worn. Her gaze scooted a little higher, to no-man's land where she either had to look at his fly or his bare chest or his face. In one visual gulp, she took in all three, then ducked her head again as he knelt beside her.

He picked up a tea bag, the tags dangling. "That's okay."

"Gee, thanks for your permission."

He ignored her weak attempt at sarcasm. "I knew you wouldn't turn me in, Mackenzie. You're the only person I've ever been able to count on."

She started to protest, then remembered his parents—one absent, one "crazy." His sister had moved away from home as soon as she'd graduated high school. Mackenzie had always sensed how alone he was beneath his tough independence.

"But you haven't seen me in ten years," she said. He'd gone ten years with no one to believe in?

While he didn't actually smile, his eyes crinkled, so she counted that as a sign of rapport. The fear inside her eased by another degree. This was Devlin, after all, who'd been nice to her even though they made the most incongruous high-school couple since Angela had fallen for *her* bad boy on *My So-Called Life.*

*My so-called crush,* Mackenzie thought, her bare feet cold on the linoleum as she leaned toward him with her heart beating in her throat. Her bruised lips had a will of their own and they were saying, "Kiss me again."

Devlin merely dropped the tea bag into the box and tilted back on his heels. "You haven't changed."

Heat spilled into her cheeks. Hadn't changed? Was he blind? For the past three months, she'd done nothing *but* change.

"That was a compliment," he said, reading her face.

"Would *you* think it's a compliment?"

Grooves appeared in his cheeks. More of a grimace than a smile, but getting closer. "It's been said about me often enough. I'm as much trouble now as I was then."

She let out a breathy snort. "More."

He disregarded that, because how could he argue? They picked up the remainder of the tea bags and stuffed them into the box, their hands colliding. She made a panicky sound in her throat when she swallowed, waiting for him to stand aside. Her rump was pressing into the cabinets.

Devlin's hand rose to the side of her face. She was aware of the heat of it, but he didn't quite touch her, except for one fingertip that stroked a lock of hair curling near her ear. "You cut your hair."

She cleared her throat, daring to look at him. "Yes. That's one change."

"Only an outward one."

Presumptuous. "But that's the only type you can see. You don't know me, after all. It's been ten years."

"You keep saying that, but it makes no difference to me." For what seemed like a long time, he simply looked at her, silently searching her face until she dropped her lashes. Her brief flare-up of defiance flickered like a weak candle flame.

He was right, the smug bastard. She hadn't changed since high school, in regards to him, anyway. She was still the same sucker, willing to risk her record and reputation—and now even her life, if that wasn't too dramatic—for Devlin Brandt. She was *such* a push-over.

He took his hand away. She resisted following it, wanting to bury her face against his shoulder and feel his arms go around her. Hold him, hug him, smell him...

She inhaled, dragging air through her nostrils. Soap and water, damp denim, male skin—so much skin. His bare chest seemed immense, swells and hollows the color of pale sand filling her field of vision like the desert did to a Bedouin. Devlin was only slightly heavier than he'd been in high school, but not as scrawny. There were thick bands of muscle beneath the mat of curly brown chest hair that had grown in since then. His stomach was ribbed with more muscles, his arms grown sinewy.

He was a man now. She wouldn't have believed it possible, but his virility had doubled. And he was doubly right—she was as susceptible to him as ever. Being near him was dizzying.

*Move away*, she thought, her own joints frozen. Even though it had been only seconds, it seemed as if they'd been kneeling on the floor forever.

"Cute," Devlin said. "But I liked your hair better long."

"It'll grow," she blurted, when she should have been sassy like Sabrina and said, "Aw, shave me," or "Yeah, well, that's some look you're sporting, rattail."

Devlin stood. Mackenzie flopped down on her rear end in relief, her gaze snared on him like a fish hook. Now that he'd straightened, she could see that he'd washed the blood from his injury. The area around his ribs was raw and red, beginning to purple into deep bruising that must hurt like the dickens.

"I can tape your ribs," she said. Her tongue was gritty, her voice as dry as powder. All the moisture in her body had pooled between her thighs.

"Thanks." He extended his right hand, taking hold and pulling her to her feet with barely a wince. His grip was one notch away from tight, but he let go easily enough when she slid her hand out of his. Goose bumps popped up on her arms.

The kettle whistled.

"That's the water for our tea." She turned, biting her tongue at the inanity.

He sidled up to the counter, his hand splayed across his ribs. "I wonder if..."

She guessed. "You're hungry? I can make you a sandwich."

He watched her pour steaming water into mugs. He hesitated. "If it's no trouble."

"No big deal. I'm hap—" Gad! She stopped, setting the kettle on the stove, forcing aside her Happy Homemaker tendencies. "It's a little late to worry about causing me trouble."

Too late for her. Devlin knew she was pushover. "Thanks," he said. "You're a peach."

*Soft and overripe*, she thought, dunking the tea bags. "Sweet."

Her head snapped up. "What?"

"I like my tea sweet. Do you have any honey?"

Blushingly remembering his sweet tooth—they'd met in ninth grade over a butterscotch candy, after all—she indicated a cupboard with a wordless nod. She spooned up one sodden tea bag and wrapped the string around it, watching him through her lashes as he reached for the honey bear squeeze bottle. *Devlin Brandt was half-naked in her kitchen.*

*He was spending the night.*

Aside from being accosted on her doorstep and having mysterious men lurking about, this was the stuff of fantasies. If she had the courage of her conviction to change, she'd seize the day. Or night, technically.

*Carpe...nox?* What the heck was Latin for night?

Bah. Forget that. *Carpe* Devlin Brandt.

If that wasn't the craziest idea she'd ever had. And if she dared.

"Do you think maybe you should tell me what's going on with you?" she asked in a struggling-for-everyday-conversation voice. Keeping her expression bland, she crossed to the fridge and took out the corned beef and pickles she got at her favorite deli. She added mustard, mayonnaise, lettuce and Swiss cheese and got a ripe red garden tomato from the basket on top of her fridge.

Devlin eased one hip against the edge of the counter and stirred honey into his tea. "We're not holding a coffee klatch, darlin'."

"And my apartment isn't a hideout...Baby Face."

He cocked a brow, stretching the skin around his blackened eye. "Baby Face?"

She shrugged, taken by the ruggedness of his features, barely distracted by the scrapes and bruises. Even in high school, Devlin couldn't have properly been called Baby Face. "He's the only gangster I could think of. I'm not so quick with the clever comebacks."

"You're too forthright."

"Too dull, you mean." Mr. Dull had always been Sabrina's nickname for Mackenzie's previous boyfriend, Jason Dole. Mackenzie had never bothered pointing out that she was custom-made for the role of Jason's wife. Until their parents' wedding and the pact they'd struck on a whim, she'd expected, in a comfortable someday-in-the-future way, to eventually reach the point where she'd be satisfied with the appropriate match she and Jason had made. Mr. and Mrs. Dull.

Jason had expected the same. He was having trouble believing that they were irrevocably broken up.

Devlin sipped the hot tea. "Mack, I've never thought of you as dull."

*Mack.* She didn't relish the reminder of their buddy-buddy past. Even though the familiarity of the name also gave her a wee frisson of pleasure.

"Sure." Briskly she made the sandwich, standing with one foot on top of the other. "I'm positively a thrill a minute."

Unless she was mistaken, Devlin's glance touched her body. "I can think of ways to make that true," he said quietly.

First the kiss, now this. Was he coming on to her?

The possibility made her shiver.

"You're cold," Devlin said. "Why don't you take your tea and go put on some socks or slippers?"

This was nuts, talking with Devlin about sandwiches and socks. Practical matters, she told herself, summoning up her usual fall-back tendency toward order and routine. She handed him the sandwich plate. "I have to take care of those ribs of yours. That bruise looks bad. It's going to get worse."

"It can wait." He lifted a corner of the bread and was apparently satisfied with her ingredients because he bit into the sandwich. "Go on. Let me eat."

Practical matters, she repeated. The bane of her existence, before tonight. Only as she left the room did she realize how neatly he'd sidestepped her questions yet again. That was par for the course. Devlin had never been one to let himself get pinned down.

"WELL, THAT SHOULD DO IT." Mackenzie smoothed the end of the tape she'd wrapped around the batting cushioning his ribs. "How do they feel? Bandage wound too tight?"

He took a breath, not too deep. "No, it's good." Earlier, he'd gulped down three extra-strength pain tablets from her medicine cabinet. The throbbing in his side had been reduced to a steady but manageable ache.

Mackenzie had cleaned his wounds with iodine and slapped Band-Aids on his chin and elbow, then tended the ribs with an earnestness that brought up memories of her scowling over his half-done homework and scolding him for smoking away his study period. Throughout the procedure, she'd seemed to believe his silence was stoic, when he was actually experiencing a pleasant buzz because he'd been fed, the living room was warm, and she'd been circling around him, leaning over into his face. Although her sweater was baggy, it rounded in all the right places. And she smelled good. Not like a perfumey flower garden, but like a clean, pure, moral woman, who was still as sexy as hell. He didn't find many of those in his line of work.

She switched off the overhead light, leaving only

the sofa lamp on, and went over to the window to check the street for the tenth time.

"See anything?"

"No. The cops must have scared them off."

A patrol car had cruised the street a couple of times, about ninety minutes after she'd made the call, so it was fortunate he and Mackenzie hadn't been in the middle of an emergency. Sloss and Bonaventure hadn't shown since. Mackenzie seemed relieved. Devlin knew better. They'd only gone underground; they hadn't given up. Come morning, he intended to sneak out of the neighborhood, but he'd have to be very careful. Any number of Fat Man's crew might be called in to run surveillance on the block during the night.

"You should get some sleep," Mackenzie said.

"You, too," he said.

She stood in the middle of the room, watching him with an expression that wavered between attraction and awe. Not necessarily a good kind of awe. Although she wasn't as wary as she'd been earlier, she wasn't treating him like a good old friend, either. No reason she should, of course.

Except that he'd missed her. Astonishing to realize just how much.

Mackenzie gave herself a shake and bustled out of the room, returning seconds later with an armload of bedding. A fat pillow was tucked under her arm. She dropped the stuff on the couch opposite his armchair.

"Maybe I should sleep out here. You'll have more room in my bed."

"No. I shouldn't be moving around much anyway—better for the ribs. And I can watch the door from here."

Her lashes batted, too many times. She was nervous. "Do you think they'll come back?"

"Probably not," he answered easily. He'd believed that her jumpiness came from residual traces of chemistry combusted by their kiss, but maybe it was only the circumstances. She'd faced Sloss down at the door with an admirable courage, but that didn't mean she wasn't frightened. He'd put her through a lot. Most of it more serious than a kiss, even an incredibly hot kiss.

"What's the game plan?" she asked, smoothing and tucking sheets over the cushions of her floral sofa.

"Pardon?"

"Am I going to wake up in the morning and find you gone?"

"Could be."

"Uh-huh." She punched the pillow. "Just like old times."

"What do you mean by that?"

"I'm not seventeen. I won't cover your butt with the principal this time."

"I don't want you to do a thing for me—after tonight."

"What if they come back to ask me more questions?"

*Or worse.* If Devlin slipped out of their reach, next

time Sloss came around he wouldn't be *asking*. The scarf, combined with Mackenzie's delay in answering the door, was already enough to make them suspicious of her. A flimsy clue, but one they'd latch on to if there was nothing else to go on.

"As far as they're concerned, you know nothing," he said.

"True." She unfolded a girly pink flannel blanket. "As far as I'm concerned, too."

That wasn't entirely true. Even though she believed he was a lowlife scum bag, she knew enough about him to put her in danger. But how could he protect her when staying, and being identified, would make it even worse for her?

All right. He was down to his last option. As soon as she went to bed, he'd have to call Lieutenant Jakes, his supervisor in the department. Deep cover work meant that contact between Devlin and the police force was kept to a minimum. His handler facilitated all evidence drops and monitored his progress. But this was a unique situation. Mackenzie, an innocent civilian, had become involved. And Jakes needed an update anyway, now that the cracks had widened and the operation was starting to crumble.

Devlin leaned forward, intending to rise until a stabbing pain stopped him. Which sucked more—cracked ribs or a cracked case?

Suddenly Mackenzie was there, steadying him with a supportive arm. "You really ought to see a doctor."

"Tomorrow," he said, to get her off his back.

"Should I help you into bed?"

He patted her arm. "No, thanks. I'm not an invalid."

She blinked, lifting her chin. "Is this it, then?"

Her eyes were like pools of melted chocolate, warm and glistening. He saw the longing in them, recognized it as no more than an echo of her old crush, and even so, he wished that he could share a moment of honesty with her. Be straight. And real. Tell her how much she meant to him, no matter how many years had passed.

But he couldn't.

"This is it," he said, not too surprised when his voice cracked, too.

She bowed her head. Crossing her arms tightly around her midriff, she kept her head low as she walked out of the room. "Goodbye, Devlin."

"'Night," he said, turning away so he wouldn't keep watching her go. After a brief hesitation, her bedroom door clicked shut and he let himself breathe again.

THE VOICES didn't wake Mackenzie as much as her restlessness. She'd drifted into an uneasy sleep after a good hour of tossing and turning and thinking of Devlin, and had awakened several times. This time, though, she heard voices.

*One* voice, she realized after sitting up in bed to listen.

She glanced at the luminous numbers on her

clock—3:26 a.m. And Devlin was talking on the phone. Everything the man did was suspicious, but there could be no normal reason for this one. Otherwise he'd have made the call earlier. All he had to do was ask for privacy.

*What did you expect? He's a criminal on the run.*

She'd have liked to be able to believe in his innocence, but that was impossible. He'd never been purely innocent in all the time she'd known him. There had been instances where he wasn't guilty, like the vandalism thing, and that was why she'd agreed to be his alibi. Their school had been broken into and trashed one night after a basketball game. The next day, police had arrived to interview students about their whereabouts. Devlin had asked her to say they'd been together. Not because he was guilty of the crime, but because he'd been out riding his motorcycle even though he'd lost his license.

Not innocent, not guilty. That was Devlin.

And she'd been so smitten with him that she'd been thrilled to be his accomplice, even if lying to the police had given her such a stomach ache she'd missed school the next day. A week later, she'd become so paranoid and guilt-ridden that Devlin had finally confessed his actual location to the police just to relieve her misery.

And then she'd felt even more miserable for letting him down.

Mackenzie made a face at herself in the dark. A real staunch supporter, she'd been, although Devlin hadn't seemed to mind her attacks of good-girl-aphobia.

She slid out of bed, searching for her scuff slippers with her toes. She was going to eavesdrop, and she didn't want Devlin to hear her moving about. Even if he needed serious help and had no one else to turn to, he also had plenty of reason to keep her out of his current trouble.

Avoiding the creaky spot in front of the door, she stepped to the side and pressed her ear against the wood. Devlin's words remained indistinguishable. The apartment was old enough to have solid oak doors, and her overnight guest was speaking in a hushed voice.

A familiar cautious voice inside her warned that she'd be better off without knowing, but she cracked the door anyway. Ms. Cautious had already cost her a fantasy night with her high-school crush. When he'd kept his distance, she'd been too timid to seize anything but another pillow from the linen closet.

"What should I do with the ruby?" Devlin was saying in a strained whisper.

*Ruby!* Mackenzie peered from her bedroom. She couldn't tell exactly where his voice had come from, and there was only a narrow slice of the darkened living room visible. She picked out the end of the couch. The bedding was thrown back. No Devlin.

She inched the door wider, looking toward the end of the hall. No lights burned in the kitchen except the small pinpoint light on the stove clock. Wherever he'd gone, he was in the dark.

He said something about a hiding place.

*Her apartment?*

"...not enough proof to make the case."

*Against whom? Devlin himself? His assailants?* She shivered. Her houseguest's one-sided conversation might be telling her nothing of substance, but it was raising the hackles on her neck.

"Give me another week, and I'll have the Fat Man's balls in a vise. Then the missing ruby will be the least of his troubles."

Mackenzie drew back. Her stomach cramped up at the dreadful thought—Devlin was a thief and he'd stolen a ruby. The two guys who'd pretended to be the police were after him. To get it back? Perhaps, although they didn't look like honest types themselves. Maybe they'd been hired. And Devlin couldn't fence the ruby until he'd lost them. Or distracted them.

Pure speculation on her part. But what else could she think?

All she knew for sure was that she didn't want Devlin to be hurt or killed. If he was a thief, he could make restitution, take his punishment. She'd try to talk him into that, but she wasn't ready to turn him in. Not yet.

In the past, for all his misdeeds, Devlin had always maintained a sort of honor. Back then, she'd believed that he was good at heart, but crying out for guidance. Now, she didn't know him well enough to say.

Her instincts were too caught up in animal attraction to be reliable.

Suddenly Devlin walked into view, his head down but nodding, the cordless phone from her living room at his ear. His hair was standing on end and he wore nothing except the binding around his rib cage and a pair of white Jockey shorts that gleamed like a flag of surrender—hers—in the darkened living room. He stopped in the open doorway. "What about the girl? She can't be harmed."

*That would be me.* Mackenzie shrank back from the door, narrowing its opening.

Devlin's head came up. She stopped breathing.

"I have to go," he said, very softly.

She put her eye to the crack. He was walking down the hallway, his jaw set.

Knowing she couldn't shut the door without him seeing, she left it and made a flying leap across the room to her bed, hoping the jouncing of the mattress would sound like the normal movements of a restless sleeper.

She plopped down and scrambled through the covers, pulling them up to her chin an instant before Devlin pushed her door open. She lay still, her heart pounding, her lungs seized up. He was looking at her—she could feel it. And, oh, God, she needed to breathe!

She let out an exhale that she tried to conceal as a sleepy groan, turning onto her side at the same time and burrowing her face into the pillow. Her nostrils flared, sucking in oxygen.

A minute passed like an hour.

"Mackenzie?" Devlin whispered.

She didn't respond.

Seize the coward.

# 4

MACKENZIE HAD JUST emerged from the bathroom and was creeping along the hallway, intending to sneak into the kitchen to make coffee, when the doorbell rang. She dashed to reach the door before Devlin was wakened. Incredibly enough, he hadn't split yet. He was sleeping, lying face down on the couch, his left arm hanging off it, knuckles dragged on the carpet. The sheet and blanket were rumpled around his middle, and she'd spent a good five minutes staring at his broad shoulders and the soles of his feet before she'd broken from her trance and gone off to take a shower. Not a cold one. Only in dire circumstances would she give up hot showers. Lusting after Devlin was divine, not dire.

She checked the peephole, then slipped off the chain, turned the locks and eased the door open. "Thank heaven it's only you."

"You were expecting the mayor?" Garbed in hot rollers and a silk leopard-print robe, Blair Boback thrust her face past the doorjamb. Blair was six feet tall, the perfect height to see over Mackenzie's head into the apartment. "Have you got someone in here?"

"Yes."

"Ooh." Blair breathed the word with husky vibrations. "Someone from the reunion?" She pushed at the door. "Has to be Devlin Brandt. You wouldn't take anyone else home."

Mackenzie held her place. "Devlin wasn't at the reunion."

Blair stopped, peering down into Mackenzie's face. "He wasn't? Damn that boy. But then who do you have inside? I knew there was something going on when you called last night—"

"Shh." Mackenzie put a finger to her lips. "You'll wake my guest." Blair's deep voice was professionally trained and carried as far as a man's.

"It's not a man?"

Mackenzie smiled. "No, it is."

"Girl! What *have* you done?"

"I can't tell you now. It's rather complicated."

Blair's gaze shot above Mackenzie's head again. Her eyes widened until white showed all around the irises. "And it's also standing in your hall half nekkid."

Mackenzie didn't turn. She grimaced.

"Mmm-hmm. Come to mama," Blair said in a rich, rolling contralto.

"Get in here." Mackenzie grabbed Blair's hand and pulled her uncensored neighbor inside before one of the upstairs tenants came down and got curious. The entire building would boil with rumors of a kinky *ménage à trois* when the truth was that Mackenzie would be thrilled to achieve some simple one-on-one action.

She took her time, conscientiously locking all the locks and sliding the chain into place, stalling the explanation because there was no explanation. For none of them, it seemed.

Finally she turned. "Blair Boback, meet Devlin Brandt."

"Hell-ohhh," Blair purred, oozing flamboyance from every pore as she toyed with the black marabou feather trim on her robe. She cocked one long bare leg in a Miss America pose, sans high-heeled sandal. Her toes were painted with neon-green glitter.

Devlin didn't speak, just gripped his sheet a little tighter. He seemed stunned.

Blair didn't take her eyes off Devlin. "I thought you said he wasn't at the reunion."

"He wasn't—"

Devlin interrupted. "We hooked up afterward." He aimed a sexy, private smile at Mackenzie that gave her a spark even though she knew it was all for Blair's benefit.

"Oh, really? Why, you little minx." Blair continued to stare at Devlin the way a dieter stares at a hot-fudge sundae, but Mackenzie thought the comment was probably meant for her. With Blair, one couldn't be sure.

The bigger question was why Devlin wanted to mislead Blair into thinking they'd slept together. She already knew why the idea gave *her* a goose, but she suspected Devlin had other motives.

"The two of you did a lot of damage," Blair commented, taking in Devlin's bruises and bandages. "I'm surprised I didn't hear screams and thuds through the walls." She winked. "Mackenzie, honey, has no one ever told you that if you break your toys, you can't play with them again?"

"It wasn't—" The look in Devlin's eyes stopped Mackenzie's denial. She glared back at him, feeling hot and flushed—and oddly flattered. "I'll be sure to let him heal before the next go-round."

She was nearly certain that Blair wasn't swallowing this. Blair knew her; they'd been neighbors for several years. But Blair would play along.

"This has been fun," Devlin said, "but I've got to go. Ms....Boback, was it? If you'll excuse me?"

"You can call me Goddess," Blair trilled as Devlin backed off down the hallway toward the bathroom. "My stage name. Goddess Galorious."

Devlin stopped. His stare scraped up and down Blair's long legs, stunning figure and sculpted face.

Mackenzie, who'd darted into the living room, handed him his jeans. "Blair is one of the stars in a drag show at the Pink Banana," she explained, taking pity on the guy.

"An *extravaganza*," Blair corrected with a toss of her hot-rollered head. The effect worked better when her hair was down—in all its shining, bouncy, auburn, wavy, waist-length glory.

"Oh." Devlin's face had gone blank. "Great. I'll, uh, see ya around." He ducked into the bathroom.

Mackenzie looked at her friend, who was shaping

her breasts and hips through the silk robe. Blair did her toothiest Goddess smile. "Don't you love it when men get that dumb-as-a-box-of-rocks expression on their faces?"

DEVLIN WAS HOPING that Mackenzie would get her nosy neighbor out of the apartment before he emerged from the bathroom, but there was only so much time he could afford to waste. He went to the bathroom quickly and washed as best as he could around the bandaged ribs, checking his watch every couple of minutes or so. He'd overslept. It was almost eight, early for visitors but late for a clean getaway. The pills he'd taken last night had knocked him out but good. He checked the bottle in the medicine cabinet. Tylenol PM. *Damn.*

Now he had this Blair or Goddess person to worry about, on top of watching Mackenzie's butt. The call to Lieutenant Jakes hadn't helped matters any, either. Devlin's superior didn't particularly want to hear about the complications, although he'd be fast to pull Devlin out of the case if he was in serious danger of getting "burned," or identified as law enforcement.

Devlin believed that the ruby he'd plucked from the thieves' stash was extremely hot. Although pried from its setting, the gem matched the description of a set of ruby jewelry recently lifted from a Park Avenue penthouse. He already had enough evidence on Sloss and Bonny and the rest of the theft ring to put them away. What Devlin needed was a way to tie the stolen goods directly to Boris Cheney, or else Fat Man's high-priced lawyers would claim their client had no knowledge of the illegal activities. In actuality, Cheney was the mastermind of the crime ring that had spread from the city and into the suburbs via his pawnshops. Three months ago, Devlin had entered the tight circle of crooks, playing an undercover role as the sort of penny-ante thief he might have become if his life had played out differently.

He'd been arrested a few months shy of his eighteenth birthday, the result of a drunken brawl. The charges had eventually been dropped, but an officer named Don Richards had read him the riot act—nothing new—and from then on had taken a personal, continuing interest that had ultimately changed Devlin.

But all that was a lifetime ago, he thought, closing the mirrored door of the cabinet. He was as disconnected from those memories as he was from the real Devlin Brandt. It was lonely being an undercover cop, particularly one who lived his cover continuously. By all accounts, he was scum. For their safety, he'd disassociated from his family. He had no friends, only acquaintances. Idiots like Bonaventure, or the informants he'd flipped. No women, at least not nice ones. He didn't even have himself.

Being with someone who'd known him in his previous life was bringing back old memories with a vengeance. Even this brief taste of a normal domestic life was intoxicating. And Mackenzie, sweet Mackenzie...

He wanted to be her hero. But he wasn't. While she

might be kind to him, even attracted to him, eventually she'd give up on him in disgust. She'd come to see what everyone else already knew—he was no damn good.

Devlin tested his sore ribs, wincing at the pain even though it had diminished. Slightly.

There was no way he could tell Mackenzie the truth, so he was stuck between a rock and a hard place on all sides. Protecting her would mean staying with her—a dangerous option when he had a strong hankering for her. Not to mention a false identity to maintain and the criminals on his tail.

What he needed was a disguise so he could come and go even if Sloss and Bonaventure were watching the building.

Devlin checked his watch again, then listened at the door. The neighbor woman—man—was still out there. Great legs, whichever sex. If only *he* could fool the eye as well....

*Hmm. That was a thought.*

"Forget it," he told his reflection. "I am not dressing up as a woman."

But that wasn't the only option, was it?

He shook his head, figuring Bonny had slammed his skull one too many times on the cement floor, but the idea didn't go away. If it worked, he'd kill two birds with one disguise—staying under Fat Man's radar while he worked his connections and wrapped up the case, and keeping close to Mackenzie to ensure her safety.

"Freakin' crazy," he said out loud, leaving the bathroom fast before he changed his mind.

Mackenzie and the man who looked like a gorgeous woman were in the kitchen, drinking coffee at a wrought-iron ice-cream parlor table. Mackenzie appeared worried, but Blair was full of it. "We thought you'd escaped through the window," he said. "I've been known to scare off my share of suitors, but Mackenzie's not used to hers disappearing so quickly. In fact, we still haven't gotten rid of Jason."

"Jason, huh."

"Mackenzie's ex." Blair tweaked a drooping tulip in the vase that sat on the table. "These flowers are from him."

Mackenzie shook her head. "Stop it, Blair. Devlin doesn't care about that."

"But I do," he said. He had to know who was a regular visitor, that's why. Right-o. Yeah, sure.

"Don't bother, Devlin." Mackenzie shrugged regrettably. "I'm afraid Blair's not buying your sleep-over-date act."

"Yeah, I doubted that," he said. "But I had to take a shot."

"It's not that a liaison would be impossible to believe," Blair said, sliding her, or maybe his, eyes—exotically amber, almond-shaped, with the kind of long lashes many a woman curled for—between Mackenzie and Devlin. "But I'm picking up falling-in-lust vibes, not give-it-to-me-one-more-time vibes."

Devlin shuffled his feet, not sure what to say to *that*. Especially since it was true.

Mackenzie stood, her face flaming. "Uh, want some coffee? You can have my seat." There were only two chairs.

Blair reached out a long bare leg and patted the seat with her—uh, *his* bare foot. "Sit here, sugar."

"I'll stand, thanks," Devlin said, backing off. He moved again to give Mackenzie access to the coffee-maker on the counter.

She handed him a cup, stopping to scope out the purple bruises that were deepening and creeping past the bandages around his ribs. "I'm sorry. I couldn't get the blood out of your shirt. But I'm sure I have a T-shirt that would fit you."

"I'd offer a piece of my clothing," Blair said, "if I wasn't so sure that you'd say no to sequins."

The perfect opening. Devlin took the plunge. "Don't bet on it."

There was a moment of stunned silence before Blair's brows arched toward his wig. "Oh? I'd never have pegged you as a cross-dresser."

"I'm not. But I need a disguise."

Mackenzie leaned back with arms akimbo, gripping the edge of her counter. "I get it. You have to get out of the building without being recognized—"

Blair clapped. "Howdeedo, *Birdcage!* I have a pair of mules you might be able to squeeze into. So what if your heels hang out the back? And a caftan would work if we gave you some padding underneath.

Maybe a turban. No, I think not. Far too Cleo from the Caribbean."

Devlin put up a hand. "Wait, wait. I am *not* dressing as a woman."

Blair's face fell. "But that's no fun."

"This isn't for fun."

"I must dissent. Everything's for fun. Life's a bowl of cherries. Else what's the point?" Blair countered.

"What do you do with the pits?" he asked, though it was an absurd discussion. But then he was having it with a drag queen and a candy impresario who obviously had little experience with the criminal element. He wanted to keep it that way.

Blair pursed his lips. "I spit them out."

"And who cleans them up?" Devlin asked. *Me*, he thought.

"This isn't getting us anywhere." Mackenzie, at least, knew the seriousness of the situation. "What kind of a disguise were you thinking of, Devlin? A baseball cap? Sunglasses?"

"More than that." He brushed his knuckles over the layers of batting at the edge of his bandages. "Something semipermanent."

"But—" Mackenzie frowned. "Once you're away..."

Devlin cleared his throat. "I've been thinking." He glanced at Blair, who'd sat back, one leg slung over the other, a bare foot swinging. Damn. The drag queen was good. Even without full makeup, he appeared one-hundred-percent female.

Devlin refocused on Mackenzie. "I know I said one night, but..."

Her knuckles whitened. "You need to stay longer?"

"That might be a good idea."

"I don't know."

"It's for—" Devlin broke off. He couldn't say it was for her protection; that would blow his cover as a common criminal. Better to play on her sympathy. "You'd really be helping me out of a tough jam."

"Then why the disguise? You could stay inside the apartment until—" She stopped and blinked. "Um, Blair, maybe you could go back to your place and round up some supplies? In case we need them."

Blair stood, moving so close to Devlin he could smell the other man's perfume. "Like what?" Blair said, looking Devlin over. "I have high heels and lace Wonderbras. This one—" a long glittery fingernail touched Devlin's cheek "—is protective of his masculinity."

"Guilty," Devlin said with a grin. "When it comes to you."

Blair laughed. "You have no idea, hon."

Mackenzie gave her neighbor a small push. "Go on, Blair. Use your imagination. I've seen your closet. It's like a department store. You'll think of something."

"Peroxide?" Blair said, and sashayed out of the room. "I'll be back in ten minutes. I love a craft project!"

Devlin waited until Mackenzie had come back from

locking the door before he blurted, "You mean to say that's a *man?"*

"I did not."

"Yes, you did." Devlin set down his coffee cup. "Blair works at the Ripe Banana—"

"The Pink Banana, yes. But I never said Blair's a man."

"Drag queens usually are."

"Usually."

"Then he's…half and half?"

"No. She's all woman." Mackenzie dimpled. "It's a Victor/Victoria kind of setup."

"I'm not following…"

"A woman pretending to be a man pretending to be a woman. Or is it a man pretending to be a woman pretending to be a man?"

Devlin shook his head. "Either way, you're saying Blair is a woman. Born that way and stayed that way, without hormones or plastic surgery?"

"Right. But the people at the drag show believe she's a man. Playing a woman."

"I see. Isn't that fraud?"

Mackenzie shrugged. "Yeah. Blair wouldn't have done it if she hadn't been desperate. She's a performer, but jobs were scarce and since she's always had this drag queen look about her—with the height and the flamboyance… Well, you know how it goes."

"Sure."

*"You're* being a stickler about fraud?"

"No, it's okay with me. I'm not involved. And, uh, PC or not, I'm much relieved."

"Because she was turning you on?"

"Not exactly." Devlin gave Mackenzie a quick scan. While he'd been in the bathroom fretting, she'd changed into a trim business suit and a pair of plain shoes with modest heels. Nothing sexy about the outfit except the body wearing it.

Mackenzie snorted and stroked her fingers through her short dark hair, smoothing it behind her ears. "I saw how you were looking at her."

"I'll admit that it was strange thinking that a man could be so gorgeous."

Mackenzie let out a small sigh. "Wait'll you see Blair dressed up, with her hair down."

He moved toward her, drawn like a magnet despite his action being a major indiscretion of his position as a cop. He touched her shoulder. "You never told me why you cut your hair, Mack."

"Does that matter? Maybe I did it years ago."

"Did you?" He didn't wait for her answer. "I saw you a couple of times, you know. In Scarsdale. Once at the market. You bought yams and a fashion magazine and a bag of butterscotch candies. It was Thanksgiving, you were probably home from college." He moved his hand to the back of her neck, sliding his fingers up into her hair like the ruff of a dog. She didn't speak, just elongated her neck, pushing against his palm. Her breathing quickened. "And then, a couple of years later. You were coming out of a movie theater with your mother. It was summer and you were wearing one of those flimsy cotton dresses that show the shape of your legs. That was...mmm." He massaged her scalp. "Your hair was still long, but all pulled back. It looked like a horse's tail."

"Why—" She licked her lips. "Why didn't you say hello?"

The first time, he'd been twenty and still at loose ends, back home for a brief visit. She'd seemed way beyond his reach. The next time, he'd been working two jobs while he took night classes and waited for his application to the police academy to come through. He'd already known that his mentor had put out the word that he'd be right for undercover work—he had the perfect background for it, and they liked to pluck young cops fresh out of training when they still retained a civilian mind-set. So he'd told himself there was no sense in starting something with Mackenzie that he wouldn't be around to finish.

"You didn't need a guy like me in your life."

She nipped her lower lip. Her body trembled, almost imperceptibly until he pressed closer and felt the quickening tremors. "But, Devlin. I could have *helped* you..."

"I didn't want to be your project."

"What's changed?"

He stopped with his mouth an inch away from her hair. "This situation's serious. It's not a game."

She pulled away from him. "Then *tell* me about it!"

"You don't need details. If Sloss and Bonny come back—"

"Aha. You know their names."

*Damn.* "Yes."

"You three are..." She narrowed her eyes. "Cohorts?"

"In cahoots," he said with a nod, trying not to smile.

"Don't laugh at me. I overheard you on the phone last night."

He sobered up fast, making calculations on how much it was safe to tell her and where she should be misled. Lurking underneath the lies he'd have to tell was also his wish to impress her, but that he ignored. Most important of all was that she didn't suspect he was an undercover cop.

"You stole a—something valuable? And these two guys want to 'retrieve' it?"

"That might be accurate."

She gave a dubious sniff. "And suddenly you've decided that sticking around here, in disguise, is a wise choice? Pardon me, but that doesn't make sense."

"It does if you realize that I'm trying to protect you."

Mackenzie caught her breath, her head rearing back. She froze like that for an instant, then put her hand to her mouth. "I see." She stared at him, her eyes sharpening as she figured the angles. "How can you help me if they return?"

He shrugged.

Her gaze traced his bare shoulders, his bandaged

midsection, then dropped to his jeans and even his socks. He grew warm under the scrutiny. "Do you have a gun?" she asked.

"No." That was the truth. He didn't carry either ID or his department-issued weapon when he was on the job, unless he was going in wired right at the end of an operation. The Fat Man knew all the tricks and had his crew pat down newer recruits, and conduct background checks. Fortunately, Devlin's cover was rock solid.

"Promise?" Mackenzie said.

He was amazed that she trusted him. "I don't have a gun," he repeated, holding up a hand Boy Scout style.

"Because I don't believe in guns."

"You have no choice. Guns aren't fairies."

She made a face. "You know what I mean. I don't want any shooting in my house. Or fighting, either."

"What about swearing?"

"Shut up."

"Spitting?"

"I thought this isn't a joke."

"It's not." He gripped her upper arms. "I don't know what the hell I'm doing. This could be a mistake, keeping you involved. But I can't leave you on your own, especially now that you know too much." He cursed, without waiting for permission. "You could be in danger, whether I stay or go."

She moved into him, putting her hands on his chest.

"Then *stay*." Her eyes searched his. "If I'm allowed any choice about my own future, I want you to stay."

"This is so wrong," he said, and then he kissed her.

Mackenzie's mouth was soft and vulnerable—the woman had no defenses. She believed he was a thief and yet she didn't even try to pull away. Even when he tightened his hold on her and yanked her up hard against him, even when he dropped his hands to her rear end, molding her glorious curves, even when he licked his tongue into her mouth with rough, hungry strokes. She merely made a sound in her throat that sounded like, "Dev," and opened her mouth a little wider.

Lust surged through him. Strong enough to knock him off his feet...and into bed.

"Wait a minute." He moved his hands to her waist, spreading his fingers to push her away even though the sense of fullness and warmth from having her breasts pressed against his chest was the best thing he'd felt in years. She was built for comfort. He craved that almost as much as the erotic intimacy promised by her lush thighs.

Rock, meet soft place.

*Damn.*

"Forget the disguise," he said, his voice flaking like rust. "I'm out of here."

"Scared?" she said when he was halfway into the living room. Her voice was soft, but taunting. Challenging.

"Not *of* you." He clenched every muscle in his body

to keep from showing her exactly how not scared of her he was. "*For* you."

She turned, one upraised arm pressed against her breasts as she rubbed a knuckle over the scoop neckline of her top, making him want to grab her and devour her like ice cream.

"No," she said, "you're scared about what's happening between us. I don't blame you. I'm scared too. You probably know what a gigantic crush I had on you in high school. And, um, I'll admit I went to the reunion hoping you'd be there. Even so, what's scary is that it's different, now that we're adults and—and—" She started to look into his face, but her eyes seemed to catch on his mouth. "And free to act on our desires."

"Your wording is so genteel." He coughed. "I would have said boink our brains out."

A smile flitted over her lips. "Or a less alliterative version thereof."

He chuckled, but there was nothing to laugh about right now. They were caught in a deadly serious cat-and-mouse game and he had no way of knowing if she'd be in more danger with him or without him.

Without him, she'd look innocent if Sloss and Bonny returned. As long as they never knew she'd harbored him. As long as they didn't think she had details and got rough with her to get them. A major risk.

Devlin preferred the option of being there to control the situation. Problem was, he'd also have to control himself around *her*.

# 5

MACKENZIE WHISPERED into Devlin's ear. "Do you trust me?"

His green eyes blazed. "I have to, don't I?"

"After the first cut, you do." She made snipping motions with the scissors. "Speak up now or forever hold your peace."

"Would that be *p-i-e-c-e*?"

She glanced at Blair, who was across the hall, in the living room, sorting through a pile of clothes. None of them looked appropriate. "You said you don't carry a gun."

"Joking."

"Yeah, but about which?" She lifted a hank of hair and snipped it off at the roots. Obviously, getting a haircut was not as traumatic to Devlin as it had been for her. He had really nice hair, too. The previous night, it had been wet and scraggly and flattened to his skull. This morning, dry and brushed, it was the same medium chestnut brown she remembered from all those years ago—still thick and wavy, burnished gold in the kitchen's overhead light.

She worked quickly, letting the pieces of hair fall to the floor. Devlin had taken one look at the bottle of peroxide Blair had returned with and requested a shaver. He'd wanted to go bald instead of blond. Mackenzie didn't care for the idea, and Blair, as the resident costume expert, had been the deciding vote. She said a bald head wouldn't go with the look she was creating.

"I don't see why you can't just stay here in my apartment while I go to work." She tilted Devlin's head forward to snip at the back of his neck. The towel was in the way, so she rearranged it.

His shoulders shifted under her fingers. "I think I will. Today. I want to see if Sloss comes back."

"Then you don't really need the disguise."

"Well. I suppose I *might* go out."

"Don't. Stay here where you'll be safe."

"Some might say I'm making myself a sitting duck."

She sighed, and came at him from another tack. "Why would they return?"

"You acted suspiciously."

"I did not! I was very cool. Considering," she added under her breath.

"Suspicious enough to make them remember you. I should have had you answer the door on the first ring."

She straightened Devlin's clipped head and stepped back to admire her work. Not bad for an amateur. "Exactly why are they after you, again?" She wanted to see if he trusted her enough to tell her about the ruby.

Blair interrupted by coming into the kitchen holding Devlin's boots up, dirty laces trailing. "These things have got to go! Were you slopping out pigpens last night?"

He shot to his feet and grabbed the boots from her, then looked sheepish when she flung up her hands in defense. "Sorry," he said, "but I think I'll keep them."

Blair flicked a hand over her hair. "I suppose you have to. We don't have proper footwear."

"Or *im*proper," Mackenzie said.

"Then you're not counting my S&M stilettos?"

"Not for Devlin."

"Absolutely not for Devlin," he said, putting a hand inside the boots. "Remember, I'm not doing drag."

Blair caressed Devlin's chin. "You'd never pass, even cleanly shaven."

He crossed his legs and said, "You're not coming near me with a razor."

The guy was a comedian, Mackenzie thought. She watched as Blair took him by the belt loop and towed him into the living room. She wore a vintage Gucci halter top from the '70s and hot pants that showed a mile of leg. Now that Devlin knew she wasn't a *male*-female impersonator, he smiled whenever he looked at her.

"We're almost the same height, so I think these pants will fit." Blair handed him a pair of flares that were vertically striped in brown, chartreuse and powder blue. She flung aside a feather boa and a pleather trenchcoat. "And here's a T-shirt."

"It's pink," Devlin said. He tucked his boots under the couch for safekeeping. "With sequins."

"Mauve. And those aren't sequins, they're rhinestone studs. What can I say—I had a fling with a Bedazzler." Blair grinned at Mackenzie. "Studding for studs, that was my catchphrase."

Devlin was horrified. "I'm not wearing this stuff."

Blair parked her hands on her hips, looking him up and down like a little girl with a Ken doll. "Bah! Just rehinge your jaw and put yourself in my hands. I know what I'm doing. No one will recognize you after this. No freaking one. Mackenzie, hon, what did you do with that peroxide?"

"It's by the kitchen sink," she said, feeling invisible. Apparently it was her fate to be associated with cheerleaders, divas and sex bombs who hogged the limelight. Her best friend in high school had thought she was nuts for liking Devlin when there were clean-cut jocks for the taking; her college sorority roommate had been the prettiest girl on campus who frequently asked Mackenzie to be her designated driver; her sister, Sabrina, was the kind of braless bohemian whom men stopped in their tracks to watch walk down the street.

Blair was smiling at Devlin. She rubbed her hands. "Goody gumdrops, we'll do the deed in there."

"No," he said, laughing as he backed off.

She stalked him, cackling with glee when he found himself cornered by the refrigerator. She straight-armed him against the door and stretched to turn on the water. "Don't be a baby—it's only hair. Your roots will be showing in a few weeks."

"Mack, help me," he called as Blair pushed and tugged him toward the sink.

Mackenzie stood by, ready with a towel. "Don't get the bandage wet," she said, then wanted to kick herself for sounding so cautious.

Blair just laughed and ducked Devlin's head under the faucet.

"WHAT ARE YOU looking for?" Devlin asked Mackenzie. He looped his arm around hers, trying to hurry her along the sidewalk to the train station.

She was checking the gurgling gutters for her reunion booklet. Somewhere between last night and this morning, it had struck her that she shouldn't have abandoned it. She'd always been a memento saver—ticket stubs, baseball pennants, matchbooks, wedding invitations. Her apartment was stuffed with vacation souvenirs, thick photo albums and lots of other tchotchkes. To let the booklet with Devlin's photo go, she must have been really, really depressed.

Funny how life could twist when you least expect it. Thank heaven for Sabrina and the bet they'd made over their grandmother's engagement ring. Without that impetus, Mackenzie might not have undergone her top-to-bottom makeover. Then she'd have given the reunion a pass and missed the thrill of meeting up with Devlin in the dead of night.

Was she sick for enjoying her "attack"? For wanting

him to stay, no matter what laws he had broken or how much danger he'd put her in? She had a feeling that a psychologist would have a field day with her.

Devlin urged Mackenzie on, saying that the trick to hiding in plain sight was to act as normally as possible. He was escorting her to work, having decided that Blair's disguise was so good the creeps that were after him wouldn't recognize him even face-to-face.

While he looked anything but normal, Mackenzie had to agree. *She* didn't recognize Devlin and she'd watched the transformation from peroxide beginning to Bedazzling end. Fortunately, flamboyant was almost normal in New York City.

He had on his own boots and underwear. Everything else was changed. The hair had come out short and spiky with a yellowy-orange hue...except in a certain light when it had a brassy green tinge. The striped flares and girlish T-shirt contrasted with the boots and a heavy belt that was all chrome buckles, chains and black leather. Devlin had wanted to wear his leather jacket to cover up, but even after the previous night's hard rain the day was too warm. Plus the thugs might have recognized it as his. Instead, Blair had painted tattoos on his exposed forearms with body paint and a henna kit. She'd put him in a pair of sunglasses with fancy squiggles on the bright blue frames and added some thickness around his middle—a backward fanny pad—to disguise his trim midsection. A skilled makeup job worthy of even a genuine drag queen concealed the scrapes and bruises, although anyone looking close would see the black eye even under an extra-thick application of cover-up.

Privately, Mackenzie thought he looked like the majority of Blair's friends from the Pink Banana, which was to say totally, flamboyantly gay. But she'd told Devlin he was a glam rocker, not even very outrageous for her Chelsea neighborhood. A giggling Blair had tried to persuade him to use a British accent and a mincing walk, but he wasn't having it.

Mackenzie was surprised how easily he'd accepted the disguise, despite the obligatory moans and groans. That he was willing to actually go out in public was even more startling. Either he had a secret theatrical streak, or he was seriously intent on protecting her.

The threat must be real. She stopped concentrating on the rain-washed gutters and started scanning the streets.

Devlin tightened the crook of his arm, drawing her closer. "Don't be so obvious."

"You should talk."

"Walk normally, as if this was any other day."

"Yes, Elton John *always* escorts me to work."

Devlin's eyes crinkled behind the big blue glasses. Blair had given him a set of brown contact lenses to dull the color of his irises, but they remained just as compelling. "Am I making you late?"

"It's okay. Sweet Something doesn't open until 10 a.m. Earlier on weekends."

"You'll be safe there."

She nodded. "We're in the middle of Greenwich

Village, surrounded by coffee bars and art galleries. In fact..." She slowed, glancing over at him.

"What?"

"You'd fit right in. My candy store is a very colorful place. You can hang out there, if you want."

His expression got grim. "I have things to do. People to see."

Mackenzie hesitated. *And trouble to make?*

Devlin glanced behind them. "Keep walking."

Something in his tone made her want to turn, but he pressed his fingers into her arm and said, "Don't look, just keep walking." She obeyed, the hairs at the back of her neck prickling.

"Who is it?" she whispered.

"Two men in a Buick, parked near the end of your street. One's holding up a newspaper, but I think they're watching the block. I'm not sure if they're after us, specifically."

Mackenzie's pulse began to race. She slid her hand into Devlin's for reassurance.

He barely noticed. They were at the corner, waiting for the crossing sign with a small group. Mackenzie was between Devlin and the car; carefully, he peered around her. She felt him tense. "Damn, that's Bonaventure."

With an effort, Mackenzie continued staring straight ahead.

"Here's what we're going to do," Devlin said as they followed the other pedestrians into the street. His tone was almost conversational. "Forget the subway.

A taxi is safer. I want you to hail a cab straight up ahead. Don't look back or you'll draw their attention for sure—"

"You're not coming with me?"

"I'm going to circle back and make sure they're not following us."

"How can you lurk in that getup?"

"Good question. Can I have the key to your back door?"

She stopped, stalling for time while she hailed a cab with what she hoped was a casual wave. Her glance darted in the direction of the suspicious vehicle, then quickly away. She didn't see a Buick, but she couldn't stand there and gawp, to be sure.

The rush and uncertainty made her jittery. Could she trust him? Devlin was her friend—albeit one she hadn't seen for ten years—but he was also a thief.

He put her in the cab, then leaned down to look into her face. "I won't steal from you, Mack." The colored contacts didn't blur the absolute sincerity in his eyes. Nor did the bleached hair and silly garb make him any less masculine.

She flushed. "I know that. But there's a wall with a locked gate—you'll need the key for that too. And, I, uh—" Her tongue fumbled as she took the key ring from her purse, remembering how Devlin had forced his way into her apartment building less than twelve hours ago. How had she gone from that to complete trust?

Maybe not complete. She slipped the keys to the

gate and the iron-barred back door off her key ring and handed them to him, keeping the others for herself. She licked her dry lips. "What are you going to do?"

A horn honked at them. The cabbie honked back, waving out the window.

"Just a little surveillance."

"From my apartment?"

"We'll see. You go on to work. Be careful, but don't worry. It looks like they're not after you. I'll be in touch."

Did that mean he was leaving her? Just like that? Hastily she found one of her business cards and thrust it into his hand as he reached to swing the car door shut. "Please call me."

He didn't answer. He simply withdrew. But he took the card. She was counting that as an optimistic sign.

The cab pulled into traffic. The driver was asking her where she wanted to go. Mackenzie couldn't answer. Her heart was in her mouth, watching Devlin as he backed off, blending into the stream of pedestrians on the busy street. She was sure that she'd never see him again.

DUTIFUL SOUL that she was, Mackenzie went on to work, although what she really ached to do was go after Devlin. Rationally, she recognized that was the kind of thing idiot girls in movies did. They wound up blundering into a robbery or a haunted house and were held at gunpoint or ectoplasm while the hero saved the day. She was smarter than that.

And, of course, there was the little problem of not being sure that Devlin *was* the hero....

Sweet Something had been carved out of two-story storefront on Bleecker Street in the Village. She'd sunk all her savings into the place, plus then some. Although it was too early to know for certain, after only a couple of weeks in business it seemed that the candy emporium would be a success. The retro candy business that had started as a trend was now a boom, and the splashy launch of Sweet Something had garnered the business invaluable publicity. Already she'd had to hire more staff to keep up with the constant stream of customers.

After opening the doors and cash registers and checking in with her new salespeople, Mackenzie climbed the spiral staircase to her balcony office. At the top, she paused to admire the view.

The store blazed with cartoon color against a backdrop of white and high-tech chrome and steel. Aside from every candy known to humankind, she offered a small variety of beverages to enjoy at the bistro tables and chairs done in transparent Lucite candy colors like lime, tangerine and candy-apple red.

Her office was the only traditional space in the store. When she'd been selecting furnishings, she'd thought she'd be grateful to leave the loud colors and gleaming chrome and escape to an office in calming gray, with a solid cherry desk. But now it seemed all wrong.

She smiled to herself. One taste of freedom and her wild side had gone berserk. Or at least become somewhat demanding.

There were bills to settle and suppliers to call—the new line of sour suckers had been more popular than she'd expected and already needed restocking but first things first. *Girl talk.*

While she had the phone speed-dial Sabrina, Mackenzie took off her jacket, revealing a cap-sleeved shell. Her arms were still pasty white and beach season was coming up fast. The stylist she'd employed to give her the makeover she'd undertaken as a result of her bet with her sister had recommended a tanning salon, but she didn't see herself as that sort of person. When it came to beach frolics, she was a sun-hat-and-sarong, pass-me-the-SPF-50 girl.

A stranger answered the phone at Decadence, the stylish bistro where Sabrina was the luncheon hostess. Drat. Sabrina was out. No advice forthcoming from that direction, although Mackenzie could imagine what her sister would say—"Go for it, Kenzie! Live on the edge!"

But the edge was sharp, which was just dandy for Sabrina, who wore her bravado like armor. Mackenzie was more sensitive than that. She'd been able to manage the breakup with Jason only because she knew she wasn't going to hurt him...or herself.

Nothing with Devlin was negotiable. Especially not her emotions.

Where was he now? What was he doing? Her thoughts veered off into worry and she pushed them back toward business. Being goal-and-reward-oriented, she made herself work for half an hour before picking up the phone, intending to dial her apartment. Odds were slim that Devlin would answer, but it didn't hurt to try.

A knock at the louvered door stopped her. Her hopes leaped. The office had a bank of windows that overlooked the store below, but she hadn't been paying attention to the comings and goings.

"Enter," she called, rising expectantly as a man came into the room. "Oh, it's you, Kit. Hi."

"Hey, Mackenzie. Is this a bad time? You sounded..."

*Like a hopelessly hopeful romantic?*

"No, no," she said, sinking into her seat. "I'm glad to see you, Kit. I called Sabrina a while ago, in fact, but she wasn't at Decadence."

"She's off at a meeting for that charity luncheon she's handling. It's coming up fast."

"Ah." Mackenzie waved Kit to a chair. Sabrina had been inordinately pleased with the assignment. "She's really taken to her job, hasn't she? Never thought I'd see the day. I'd almost have to say she's being responsible."

"She's doing a good job." Kit Rex was Sabrina's latest beau, the most serious yet. Maybe the *only* serious one. He was devastatingly handsome, dark and brooding, with the air of a pirate about him that wasn't entirely caused by the gold hoop in his ear.

Sabrina had met Kit on the job and immediately fallen in lust. However, as part of the sisters' pact, she'd forsworn men. Mackenzie had suggested Sabrina consume chocolate every time she was tempted by Kit, but that had worked for only so long.

Long enough, Mackenzie believed—even though Sabrina hadn't admitted as much—for her sister to fall in love before she fell into bed.

Mackenzie folded her hands atop the desk. "What can I do for you, Kit?"

"It's about Sabrina," he said, looking vaguely uncomfortable.

Mackenzie blinked. "You're not going to leave her!"

"What—"

"Oh, Kit. You know how she is. Now that I've actually convinced her to stay in one place, being left is the worst thing that could happen to her. I know it was a long time ago, but she was so hurt by our mom and dad's divorce that I—"

"Mackenzie, stop." Kit was a bit taken aback by her outburst. "I'm not leaving Sabrina."

"Sorry." Mackenzie's skin crawled with embarrassment. This was why she usually kept her mouth shut and waited to figure things out before leaping in and making a fool of herself. "It's just that...well, I've always been protective of Sabrina."

"But she's the older sister."

"Only by a year. And she's much more..." Mackenzie shifted in her desk chair, trying to find the word that would explain the difference between them. "Fragile," she said.

Kit smiled. "Sabrina thinks she's tough."

"You and I know otherwise." Mackenzie took a breath, settling herself. Though it rarely happened, she could be fierce when roused. "Pardon me for jumping to conclusions. What were you going to say?"

"I have a presumptuous request."

"Of me?"

"You're involved. You see..." Kit cleared his throat. "I'm going to ask Sabrina to marry me."

Mackenzie's lips puckered into an *O*. She exhaled. "My goodness." She wasn't exactly shocked—she'd learned enough about Kit's background to know that he wanted a family. Him thinking Sabrina was ready for marriage was the kicker. "Umm, Kit. That's wonderful, but...aren't you rushing this?"

"I'm head over heels." He scratched his head, smiling a little to himself as if bewildered by how smitten he was. "We've been together for nearly..." He paused to count back. "Okay, it's only been two, three months. But that's long enough. Your sister is a potent brew."

Mackenzie grinned. "No testimonials are needed on your behalf. I'm wondering about Sabrina, though. You might have a hard time pinning her down."

"Yeah, but I've got a surprise lined up that might

convince her. Except I need something from you. Sabrina's mentioned a ring? Or, actually, I overheard her talking about it."

Suddenly Mackenzie understood. "You want the ring." Her stomach swooped.

Kit was trying to read her expression. "If that's appropriate."

Mackenzie explained. "The ring was our grandmother's engagement ring. She gave it to our mom, who passed it down to Sabrina when she and Dad got remarried. They wanted a new ring, you see..."

She wasn't sure that she should tell Kit about the bet she and Sabrina had made on the evening of their parents' recent wedding. Initially, Sabrina had tried to give Mackenzie the diamond ring on the pretext that she was dedicated to staying single and would never use it. But Mackenzie had known that Sabrina *did* care about the ring—they both did, ever since they were young girls—and in the end they'd decided that the precious heirloom would be the prize in their bet. They hadn't planned on settling up until next year, when they could assess how their life changes had gone, but events had proceeded at a much faster pace than they'd anticipated.

Mackenzie bit her lip. "Sabrina is the oldest. She should have the ring."

Kit picked up on her hesitation. "Is their some question...?"

"No." Mackenzie had made up her mind. "Having

you propose with the family ring will mean everything to Sabrina."

"I'm surprised she'd go for a traditional symbol."

"It's a girl thing. When we were small, just about every time our mom took the ring off for housework or showering or the like, we'd fight over who got to wear it. Even after the divorce, we'd sneak it out of her jewelry box and try it on. Sabrina wore it out once when she was fifteen—without Mom knowing about it, of course. I was a nervous wreck until she returned it."

Kit grinned. "At least she didn't lose it. Or hock it."

"N-n-o-o-o," Mackenzie drawled. "That ring is probably the one thing that Sabrina still believes in. Until you." Suddenly Mackenzie was struck by delight. She jumped up and went to give Kit a hug. "I am so happy for you two."

"Then you think I have a shot?"

"Sure, although you may have to do some fine talking to convince her. You could try chocolate."

"I may."

"When she moved to the new apartment, Sabrina left the ring with me for safekeeping. You know her place. I have better security...."

Mackenzie's voice died off as she realized what she was saying. *Security? She'd given her key to a man with a prison record and a penchant for jewel theft!*

"Mackenzie, you okay?" she heard Kit asking from a distance.

She walked numbly around her desk and dropped

into the chair. For all she knew, Devlin was emptying her apartment of all her valuables right this moment.

"I'm fine," she said. *Just stupid.*

"You don't look fine. Either you've seen a ghost or the ring means more to you than you're saying."

Gritting her teeth, she tried to smile at Kit reassuringly. "The ring should be Sabrina's. I'll, uh, get it from home and..." What would she say to her sister if she'd lost the ring? Sabrina would be crushed.

"I can pick it up, if you'd rather," Kit offered.

Mackenzie was thinking fast. Better not to have him come to her apartment, just in case. "No, I'll do it. As soon as I have the chance, I'll bring it to the restaurant." She crossed her fingers under the desk. "When do you need it?"

"The luncheon is next week, so not till then. I'm going to surprise Sabrina afterward, down at the seaport."

Mackenzie gave an awkward chuckle. "Well, don't let her knock you off the pier if she jumps into your arms."

Kit stood to leave. "I can only hope she gets that excited." He pushed his hands into the pockets, ducking his head down and looking at her sideways. "Thanks for offering the ring, Mackenzie. You're a gem."

At that, she almost groaned out loud. Gem*less* was a possibility. The Devlin she used to know wouldn't steal from her. But the Devlin from last night...

Mackenzie said something polite to Kit and waved

him off, feeling like an actor who'd forgotten her next line in a play with an unwritten ending.

DEVLIN MOVED his shoulders against the dank brick wall. Above, the sky was a soft blue-gray, clinging to daylight and the promise of the long summer season. The alley below was miserable—always shadowed, moist, smelly with ripe garbage, fit only for slugs and stray cats. And rats. Both the four- and two-legged kind, he thought, breathing through his mouth as he watched one scurry behind the overflowing Dumpster.

He wondered what Mackenzie was doing. She should be home from work by now. He pictured her puttering around the apartment, plumping pillows, making supper, washing dishes, settling in her chair with a book, the candy dish at hand. Safe.

She was safe, he told himself.

That morning, he'd doubled back after putting Mack into the cab, circling the block so he'd come up behind the Buick, which hadn't moved. He'd watched Bonny and his companion—one of the young punks who supplied the pawnshops—until midmorning, when they'd finally given up and driven off. That had told Devlin that Bonny was only on a fishing expedition. If there had been strict orders, he'd have applied himself. Left to his own initiative, he was a slacker.

Mackenzie was safe. Devlin was safe to return there, if he was very careful about it.

He realized he'd been turning her keys over in his

hand for the past twenty minutes and thrust them into the pocket of his jeans. Late in the day, he'd slipped into her apartment to put on his own clothes. The disguise was good for walking out in broad daylight, but he couldn't skulk in it.

Finally the back door opened and Frankie came out. Devlin waited, hidden behind a tower of pallets and cardboard cartons.

"Psst. Dev?"

He came forward, keeping an eye on the part of street visible from the alleyway.

Frankie nodded, then lit a match and applied it to the end of the cigarette hanging from his mouth. He was the bartender at the dive on the other side of door—he saw and heard everything that went on in the Lower East Side. Twenty months ago, Devlin had helped get Frankie's younger sister off the streets and the bartender had been a valuable resource ever since.

Smoke curled from Frankie's nostrils when he exhaled. "What'd you do to your hair, man?"

Devlin adjusted the do-rag so it came down lower on his forehead. "A new look."

"Yeah, you always did have a flair." Frankie was six-four and bulky, with a face that looked as if it had been made from spare parts. "Connie still has a crush on you."

"How's your sister doing?"

"Going to cosmetology school. Comes home smelling like chemicals from them perms they give."

"Could be worse. She could smell like you."

Frankie gave him a friendly sneer and kept smoking. Devlin watched the door, the street, the rusty fire escape.

"So you're in trouble again."

"You know?" Devlin squinted at the bartender through the smoke. "Have you picked up any talk?"

"Only that Sloss and Bonny are looking for you. Sloss came in late last night, spreading the word."

As Devlin had suspected. It wasn't safe for him to go anywhere familiar.

"He was planning to head up to your place, hoping you'd show, I guess. What'd you do?"

"Got caught with my hands in the cookie jar."

Frankie pinched the nub of his cigarette. "Fat Man know yet?"

"No doubt."

"I'll watch your back, best I can."

"Just keep your ears open. I'll be in touch." They shook hands, Frankie pumping Devlin's arm so he felt it in his ribs.

"Got a place to stay?" the bartender asked.

Devlin wasn't going near clingy Connie, so he said, "Yeah," even though he wasn't too sure about returning to Mackenzie's. He had other contacts to see yet tonight. Maybe something would turn up. Or maybe he'd give in and return.

He should be concentrating on making his case, and instead the thought of crawling into Mack's warm bed and holding her close was dragging at him like an undertow.

# 6

THE APARTMENT was completely empty. Mackenzie knew it as soon as she stepped inside. It took her a minute to recognize the irony.

*Empty* didn't mean burglarized.

*Empty* meant lacking. No thrill, no danger, no Devlin.

Troubled, she set her briefcase on the hall table and slipped out of her shoes. One strange night with Devlin and suddenly her home wasn't the same.

She'd lucked into this apartment straight out of college, subletting from a family friend who'd moved out of the city. The rent had been a stretch, so she'd had a roommate for the first couple of years. Then her career had progressed and she'd secured the lease under her own name when it came up. She'd been here ever since, and had devoted herself to painting, fixing, furnishing. She'd always felt safe and happy here, with her books and TV, stocked cupboards, organized closets, friends nearby but also privacy when she wanted it.

And now...

She picked up her shoes and went to the bedroom. Her jewelry box was open. She must have left it that

way when she'd raced home after Kit's visit to Sweet
Something that afternoon. She'd found the ring exactly where it was supposed to be, with no sign of
Devlin at all except for damp towels in the kitchen and
a few stray feathers from Blair's silly costumes. She'd
berated herself for not trusting him, but she'd also
taken the ring out of the box and scouted around for a
hiding place. Finally she'd shoved it into the toe of a
thick pair of folded wool socks that she tucked away
in the very back of her sock drawer.

The ring was safe. Kit would get it next week.

And at least her sister would be happy.

Mackenzie frowned. When had she gotten so
whiny?

She thought of a quote from one of her favorite romantic movies—*Snap out of it*.

Right. Such good advice she said it out loud. "Snap
out of it."

She marched to the back door that opened to the
courtyard, checking the lock. The chain was hanging
undone and she left it that way, not stopping to think
why. Briskly, she changed into a T-shirt and cotton pajama bottoms, then remembered the panty shaper
she'd shoved under the bed and had to get down on
hands and knees to retrieve it.

She took the vile garment into the bathroom, started
to drop it into the hamper and then changed her mind
and tossed into her tortoiseshell trash can instead. Her
stylist had provided good advice about makeup and
wardrobe, but Mackenzie was drawing the line at

# GET FREE BOOKS and a FREE GIFT WHEN YOU PLAY THE...

*Just scratch off the silver box with a coin. Then check below to see the gifts you get!*

## SLOT MACHINE GAME!

## YES! I have scratched off the silver box. Please send me the 2 free Harlequin Temptation® books and gift for which I qualify. I understand I am under no obligation to purchase any books, as explained on the back of this card.

**342 HDL DRRP**                    **142 HDL DRR5**

FIRST NAME                LAST NAME

ADDRESS

APT.#          CITY

STATE/PROV.          ZIP/POSTAL CODE

| 7 | 7 | 7 | **Worth TWO FREE BOOKS plus a BONUS Mystery Gift!** |
| 🍒 | 🍒 | 🍒 | **Worth TWO FREE BOOKS!** |
| ♣ | ♣ | ♣ | **Worth ONE FREE BOOK!** |
| 🔔 | 🔔 | 🍒 | **TRY AGAIN!** |

*Visit us online at www.eHarlequin.com*

(H-T-01/03)

**DETACH AND MAIL CARD TODAY!**

## The Harlequin Reader Service® — Here's how it works:

Accepting your 2 free books and gift places you under no obligation to buy anything. You may keep the books and gift and return the shipping statement marked "cancel." If you do not cancel, about a month later we'll send you 4 additional books and bill you just $3.57 each in the U.S., or $4.24 each in Canada, plus 25¢ shipping & handling per book and applicable taxes if any.* That's the complete price and — compared to cover prices of $4.25 each in the U.S. and $4.99 each in Canada — it's quite a bargain! You may cancel at any time, but if you choose to continue, every month we'll send you 4 more books, which you may either purchase at the discount price or return to us and cancel your subscription.
*Terms and prices subject to change without notice. Sales tax applicable in N.Y. Canadian residents will be charged applicable provincial taxes and GST. Credit or debit balances in a customer's account(s) may be offset by any other outstanding balance owed by or to the customer.

If offer card is missing write to: Harlequin Reader Service, 3010 Walden Ave., P.O. Box 1867, Buffalo NY 14240-1867

BUSINESS REPLY MAIL

FIRST-CLASS MAIL     PERMIT NO. 717-003     BUFFALO, NY

POSTAGE WILL BE PAID BY ADDRESSEE

HARLEQUIN READER SERVICE
3010 WALDEN AVE
PO BOX 1867
BUFFALO NY 14240-9952

NO POSTAGE
NECESSARY
IF MAILED
IN THE
UNITED STATES

girdles. There was nothing wrong with having a comfortably *zaftig* shape. Rubenesque was supposed to be "in." *Bwahahaha*.

Of course, Devlin had seemed to admire her curves.

On the other hand, she didn't know how genuine he was.

She brushed her short hair, remembering the day her sister had brought her to the salon for the radical cut. Sabrina hadn't known, but Mackenzie's plan was to snip Devlin out of her memory along with her waist-length locks. Clearly, that hadn't worked—even before he'd showed up on her doorstep.

She snapped on a headband and briskly scrubbed her hands and face even though she couldn't soap him away, either. Her life would have been so easy if she'd stuck with Jason Dole. He was her speed—slow. He was her style—comfortable.

Jason was the anti-Devlin Brandt.

But there was the pact she'd made with Sabrina. And she'd followed through on all her promises. She couldn't go back now, even without the ring at stake. For her, the pact had always been more about herself and her need to remake her staid, settled life than the heirloom engagement ring.

BLAIR WAS WORKING at the club, so Mackenzie didn't expect to hear from her, but Sabrina called minutes before bedtime.

Mackenzie had just slipped under the blankets with a bestseller she'd been reading, *Blissfully Single*. She'd picked it up because the author's name happened to be Bliss—Stevie Bliss. And because one never knew when one might need tips on how to deflect those nasty middle-of-the-night single girl blues. The author used phrases like "sizzling womanhood" and advocated enjoying men for thirty days and then throwing them away. By the time Mackenzie had finished the second chapter, she'd realized that she might as well have been getting a lecture from her sister. This Stevie Bliss woman was obviously Sabrina's lost-at-birth twin.

The phone rang. "Mackenzie!" Sabrina said when her sister picked up. "What happened? You didn't even call to tell me about the reunion."

"It was late by the time I got home." Mackenzie set aside the book and pulled the covers up to her chin. "Besides, it wasn't very interesting. I caught up with a few friends, drank punch, danced with my old science teacher, rehashed high-school days, counted pregnant classmates and came home in the rain."

Sabrina was silent for all of three seconds. "So Devlin didn't show, huh?"

"What do you know about Devlin?"

"Nothing, that's why I ask."

"I mean, why would you think—"

"That he was the person you hoped to see? C'mon, Mackenzie, you think I don't remember high school? I may have been one grade ahead of you, but we were close enough that I knew how you felt about Devlin."

"And here I thought I'd been so discreet."

"You wear your heart on your sleeve, sweetie."

"Not anymore."

"Ha! You're transparent."

"You'd be surprised how well I can keep a secret." Two of them, she thought.

The phone went silent. Mackenzie could almost feel Sabrina trying to decipher the cryptic remark. She controlled the urge to explain and felt rather pleased with herself for doing so. Sabrina would absolutely die if she knew the story of the past twenty-four hours. But Devlin was counting on Mackenzie. Even if he'd vanished from her life again, she wasn't going to betray him.

"C'mon, give," Sabrina coaxed. "What kind of secret?"

Mackenzie decided to deflect the attention. "It's not mine to say."

"Then whose?"

"No comment."

"Don't tell me. Mom's pregnant." Their parents had finally returned from a transatlantic honeymoon cruise and settled into the old family home they'd sold at the time of their divorce and had recently repurchased in an effort to make amends for their past mistakes. Both sisters felt off-kilter about that, as if they were stuck in a time warp. Still, it was very good to see their parents together.

"Pregnant at fifty? I sure hope not," Mackenzie said. "You're more than enough sister for me. I have the feeling Mom's going to be expecting grandbabies soon enough."

"You'd better get busy then."

"But you made me break up with Jason. I'm a dedicated entrepreneur now. *You*, however—"

"Ew! Don't even think it!"

"Kit would be a great father," Mackenzie said with enthusiasm. Not that she was trying to exert any influence.

Sabrina sighed. "Yeah..."

If phone lines could smile and go all moony-eyed, Sabrina's had. In fact, her vehemence had mollified so quickly that Mackenzie began to wonder if Kit's proposal had a decent chance. "Blissfully single" might become "blissfully married." Mackenzie had always imagined that she'd be the one with a husband and kids and Sabrina would fly in a couple of times a year from some exotic location, distributing presents and coochie-coos.

She might have to adjust that vision, along with the rest of her life. Okay, no problem. She'd been predictable long enough. Opening a new business and cutting her hair was only a warm-up. Now she was ready to take a real chance. She was going to throw her inhibitions away and embrace her sizzling womanhood.

*Keep telling yourself that.*

"Do you know something about what Kit's been up to?" Sabrina guessed. "He's been very secretive the past few days."

Mackenzie scoffed. "How would I? You've both

been busy preparing for the charity event." Sabrina had surprised them all with her new, responsible attitude.

"It's next week. I'm already getting a little nervous."

Sabrina nervous? "Why?"

"I don't want to be a screw-up this time."

"Not a chance. You're going to wow them."

"Kit's desserts will. I can count on that."

"Sure, but you can count on yourself, too. Don't you know that yet?"

"We'll see," Sabrina said. "I'm not like you, so assured and savvy when it comes to career stuff. I told you about the time the magician almost sawed me in half because I flubbed the trick, right?"

Mackenzie chuckled. "It's an awards lunch. No blood will spill."

"Let's hope. Well, I should go. Early morning." Sabrina didn't seem to notice how strange that was— her, heeding an early morning. "Are you sure you don't want to tell me that secret? Or give me at least a teensy hint?"

"Not on grandmother's ring."

Sabrina laughed. "When did you get so cheeky?" She hung up with promises to call again soon, but her last words were "Sorry about Devlin, sis."

*I'm not.* Mackenzie set the phone in its cradle. Sabrina had no idea how much her world was about to change in only a day—or how much her sister's also had.

Except here she was, snuggled alone in bed as if nothing had happened. Her fling with blissful single-hood aside, there was something kind of sad about that, even if she did feel different inside.

MACKENZIE DIDN'T bolt awake. She surfaced slowly, her head filled with ephemeral dreams of kisses and caresses, only to realize that she was in bed alone and her arms were wrapped around a pillow that wasn't very apt at returning affection. A dog...she should get a dog....

Even without opening her eyes, she could tell by the sounds of the city that it was deep night. Dark, endless night. Not morning, when she could return to routine and start forgetting about...

Her thoughts were jumbled, but Devlin was in every one of them. What would she do? After ten years of never seeing him, never really talking about him to a third party, she'd managed to push him to a corner of her mind, but *now...*

The dreams had stolen her defenses. The need for him was so visceral it was as if he were in the room with her.

Turning over, she let out a soft moan. And then he *was* there—a dark shape standing over her bed.

The inside of her mouth suddenly tasted like chalk. She blinked, squinted. He was gone. A figment of her imagination.

She rose up on her elbows, almost afraid to move, as if that alone would banish her to reality. But there came a soft sound, like a foot padding on the carpet, this time on the other side of the bed. Very real.

"Devlin?" she whispered, scared but then not really. By day, she had doubts. At night...

"*Shh.*"

The curtains blocked any light from outside. There was only a gold thread outlining the door she'd left slightly ajar. Devlin was a black shape, hunched beside the bed. Kneeling?

She wanted to reach out. Instead she burrowed deeper into the pillows, her fingers clenched on the top sheet that was all that covered her. "I thought you weren't coming back."

He didn't answer for a long while. Then, a sigh came from him like a sad confession. The mattress shifted as he leaned against it. "Maybe I shouldn't have."

"You're tired." She curved toward him, her body yearning, molding instinctively to his shape. He'd stretched his arms across the bed, his head resting atop them. "Sleep," she said, one hand gliding over his shoulders. She rolled closer, her cheek finding his head. The newly cut and colored hair was coarse, smelling of night air and chemicals.

"I'll go," he said, not moving except to turn his face toward hers.

Her breathing seemed to fill the room, she was so aware and aroused. "Stay." She drew him toward her.

He sighed again, deeply. His palm touched her cheek. "So warm."

"I was sleeping."

His head dropped. He inhaled. "The sheets smell like you."

He was halfway onto the bed. She was lying on her back again, one arm wound around him, her hand clasping his biceps as if that would stop him from leaving.

She was starting to think, and she didn't want to. "Come here, next to me."

Devlin lifted his face and finally she saw him, not clearly, but she didn't need to read his expression when his voice came, reaching inside her, saying so much even though his only words were "You're sure?"

She nodded, not thinking about whether or not he'd see the gesture because she knew he'd understand, and that she didn't have to speak her wishes aloud. He'd probably always known.

She reached her arms around him as his full weight settled onto the bed, wanting to feel his body pressing into hers, all of him against her, holding, covering, filling her. At last.

He'd always known. How much she wanted this.

She kissed him first. His jaw was rough and prickly but his lips were gentle and slightly parted. He let her kiss him, and in the dark she explored the shape of his lips, the texture of his tongue, the taste of his mouth. He'd been drinking. Whiskey, she thought, picturing him slouched in a dark, seedy bar where the floozies would eye him like a pot of gold.

Tonight, he was hers.

And she wasn't going to second-guess herself.

Just one tentative foray of her hand up his shirt and he stripped it off. She let out a sigh of deep pleasure as he put his arms around her. Face buried in his furred chest, inhaling his skin, she hugged him to her, lost in warmth and scent and sensation. Now she was glad it was so dark—she didn't have to worry about how whacked-out her expression must be. Her eyeballs were rolling upwards and she squeezed her lids shut, holding on to Devlin for all she was worth.

His mouth was at the side of her neck, alternately kissing and licking. She shivered against him, but she wasn't cold. A sensation like hot syrup was inching through her veins, making her skin swell and tingle, calling for his touch.

He wasn't shy, like her. He put both hands up inside her oversize T-shirt, sliding his palms across her warm abdomen, going straight for her breasts with a suddenness that stole her breath. She gasped. He gripped her firmly, kneading flesh, his fingers finding her nipples and rolling them, raking them.

Her body surged upward, heels dug into the mattress. If not for the pillows, the top of her head would have smashed into the iron bars of the headboard, but she probably wouldn't have cared. She was riding a scalding surge of rapture and it was unlike anything she'd ever experienced. She'd had good sex, pleasurable sex, but never earth-shattering, mind-blowing, better-than-in-her-dreams sex.

She knew with every pulsing cell in her body that Devlin was the man to deliver the goods.

Even if it was only once.

She banished the thought from her mind. *Don't think, don't think.*

*Feel.*

As if to make up for his caveman groping, Devlin had lowered his mouth to her bared stomach and was tracing her skin with a delicate tongue. She had an instant of self-conscious fear that he would find her too soft, too plump, but she banished that thought, too, and let herself coast on the pleasure. His hands were still playing with her breasts and seemed reluctant to let go, so he used his chin to slide the elastic waistband of her pajamas past the curve of her belly. "So warm," he said again as her thighs came up to cradle his head. His open mouth traveled over every exposed inch of skin, working its way up until she was curled into a fetal position and his nose was nudging between her breasts. He cupped them, lifting their weight so her taut nipples were pointing to the ceiling, and as his head reared back she saw the flash of his smile and was never so happy that she had sumptuous curves that pleased him.

"Finally," he said with a low growl. "Second base with Mackenzie Bliss."

A squeal of protest flew out of her mouth before she could clamp her lips shut. She slapped a hand over her eyes, sure that her blush was giving off a neon glow.

He chuckled. "And it only took me ten years to get here."

"As if you ever tried before," she said before she could stop herself, tipping up the edge of her hand to peer at him. She didn't want to be holding a conversation—she wanted to keep her eyes closed and let fantasy take over.

"Only becau—"

"Shush." She took hold of his ears and steered his head downward.

He ran his tongue along her cleavage. She made a mewling sound of approval. She shifted her shoulders and turned her head into the soft down of the pillows, blotting out the room while she waited, her breath coming in short, quick pants.

His thumb strummed one nipple while his lips closed over the other. A lick, a tug, a long, erotic pull and she was arching beneath him, her eyes squeezed shut so tightly stars burst on the inside of her lids.

"I like how you taste," he said, but his voice was far away.

She was lost in a dream. This *must* be a dream. It was too glorious, too remarkable, to be her real life.

Without a thought, Mackenzie let herself go with it. All insecurities were abandoned as she surrendered to the thrill of making love with Devlin. He was a perfect lover, knowing when to be firm, when to slow down, where to kiss and stroke and suck and how much pleasure she could take without spinning out of control. She didn't even try to keep track of time or turns or clothing that was hastily pushed aside. They were both feasting on each other's bodies in the dark, twisting, turning, tangling legs, laughing one minute and then incoherent with passion the next.

Only a few whispered words passed between them, and one breathless conversation.

Devlin paused, a hairbreadth from plunging inside her. "I almost forgot—"

She was *dying*. "I don't have any..."

"I do. Somewhere." His thick erection pressed against her belly as he reached to the floor, searching for his jeans or wallet or whatever—she didn't care even though, somewhere at the back of her brain, she was grateful that he did. A mindless need had built in her. She pulsed with it, moved with it like a tide, damp, sultry, her thighs held wide open, offering herself to him if only he would hurry...*hurry*...

She heard the snap of the condom and then finally he was back, one hand slipping over the slick skin of her inside thigh before he lifted her leg a little higher, his hand catching at the back of her knee as he pressed against her—so *big*. He entered in a slow, sure glide— so *deep*—until the throbbing inside her wasn't only her desire, it was *him*.

Mackenzie's eyes shot open.

Devlin's hands were on her thighs, then her hips, holding her up as he stroked her from the inside out. It felt just as good, but she'd lost the mindlessness. Other thoughts were crashing in, pelting questions about who he was, what was happening, how could she?

How in the world could Good Girl Mackenzie Bliss do—

The strokes had become powerful thrusts. Devlin's body strained against hers, and even in her doubt she tried to follow along. It wasn't her body hesitating, it was her head.

He breathed her name, got no reply and said it again, more sharply. "Mackenzie?"

She wound her arms around his shoulders, rocking with him as she crooned. "Mmm-hmm, yes, yes..."

He thrust into her, shuddering in climax. She wanted that, welcomed it, but he must have known that the dream had fractured because suddenly he pulled out, shoving himself away from her and doubling over as his quaking body gradually quieted.

She lay stunned, frozen in place, but reeling. Only when Devlin started to turn toward her did she move, scrambling to cover herself with the sheet. She flipped onto her side, wiggling up her pajama bottoms and then pressing her thighs tightly together, drawing her knees up toward her chest. Her T-shirt was wadded beneath her, hanging off one shoulder.

She heard Devlin pulling up his jeans and cringed, feeling furtive and guilty. Not only hadn't they looked each other in the eye, they hadn't even undressed properly.

He put a hand on her. She tensed. He stroked along her spine, up to her shoulder. Applied pressure, trying to turn her. She resisted.

"Mack..."

"Let's go to sleep," she said, her voice a little too high-pitched. She had to unscrew her face to fake a yawn. "I have an early morning."

"But..."

She tugged the sheet higher, covering her bare shoulder. Still she could feel him looking at her, thinking—oh, who knew what? Maybe that he'd given it a shot, but it wasn't his fault if she was too uptight and not worth the wait.

"Sleep," she said, cutting him off when she sensed that he was going to speak again. Damn that haircut. The back of her neck was exposed.

DEVLIN KNEW the instant Mackenzie slipped out of bed. Tired as he was, he hadn't been able to sleep with her cowering beside him. Every couple of seconds, right after she'd turned away from him, her legs had jerked with an involuntary spasm. It was a very tiny flinch, but he was right next to her—he could feel it. Hell, he could have sensed her frustration across a ballroom.

If she'd let him, he would have kept going and she wouldn't have had to suffer. Even with her head not into it, her body would have responded and let go of the tension that had built up inside her. But no way would he touch her if she was lying there cringing and embarrassed about having made love to an unworthy, lying punk.

It didn't matter that he was a cop now. She didn't know that anyway.

Or that he was supposed to be accustomed to his role as a seedy criminal. Over the years, he'd run into a few people from his hometown, especially when he'd been out in the suburbs, lurking at the Yonkers branch of Cheney's pawnshops. They'd all heard about his prison sentence, of course. Even his old friends—those who'd straightened out their act, anyway—gave him a wide berth. He'd accepted the scorn as a given when he'd signed on to undercover work, but that didn't mean it never hurt.

Maybe that was what hadn't fit and why he was still awake an hour later. Back when, Mackenzie had never acted as if she thought he was beneath her. And, of course, she had reason to doubt him now—he'd snatched her off her front stoop, for crying out loud.

If he'd been a true gentleman, he would have conceded that sex between them had been a bad idea. He'd have left her alone.

But...he wasn't ready to give up on them. Now that she was back in his life, he knew without a doubt that he wanted to keep her there. Unfortunately, with his job, that was nearly impossible. A slim chance, maybe, if he quit his present lifestyle. Until then, the best he could hope for was that she wouldn't give up and tell him to stay out of her sight forever.

She was the kind of woman who picked up strays. Even so, she had to think he might be salvageable. He couldn't spill the truth, not until he'd managed to pull together enough evidence to finish this case. So somehow he'd have to convince her to believe in him. To trust him one-hundred percent.

Obviously, she didn't—yet.

She'd curled into a trembling ball and kept quiet until she thought he was asleep, then crept out of the bedroom. She'd shut the door behind her, but a line of light showed beneath it, and he could hear her moving around. Pacing, back and forth.

He waited a while, letting her get rid of some of her pent-up energy. Then he went to make things right.

"MACK," HE SAID, right behind her.

She jumped, shrieked, flung out a hand to slap or push him. He caught it in midair.

She wrenched away. "Quit doing that to me!"

"Sorry. Didn't mean to scare you."

"Clear your throat or something. Stamp your foot. Just don't sneak up on me again."

She was talking as if he was going to be around for a while. He wondered if she realized it. He wondered if she had any idea how his heart jumped at the possibility.

"I'll keep that in mind."

"Fine," she spat, turning away and stalking into the kitchen.

She was cute in a temper. One pajama leg was pushed up to the knee, the other flapped over her heel. She huddled inside her baggy sleep shirt and a grandma sweater she'd pulled on despite the season. Her lips pooched out in a pout and her forehead was rumpled with worry. Even her short hair was cute—she kept stroking it into place behind her ears, but it was standing up on top of her head like the bristles of a porcupine.

*Bristly*, that was the word for her. But he knew the way to reach her where she was soft and vulnerable. *Candy*.

Remembering a candy dish in the living room, he went there before following her to the kitchen. She was making tea again, giving a very un-Mackenzie-like curse when she splashed steaming water on her thumb.

"You don't need tea, you need this." He opened his hand under her nose, offering her the butterscotch candies.

She hesitated. Her eyes went to his.

"Take one," he said. "Take two."

She did, unwrapping one candy and popping it in her mouth. He followed suit, slipping the remainder of the candies into his jeans pocket for future emergencies. The buttery sweetness coated his tongue as he sucked, taking away the taste of Mackenzie's mouth and Mackenzie's skin, dammit.

She didn't speak. He had to. "Are you going to tell me what happened?"

*Blink.* "What do you mean, what happened?"

"I lost you, at the end."

"I was there. Maybe I'm just not—" she inhaled "—very good."

"You were good. You were perfect. Until the end,

when your head decided to go on a little vacation from your body."

She shrugged. But her worried brow smoothed out.

"Why did you turn away? I would have made sure you were satis—"

"Why did you?" she asked fiercely, cutting him off. Her cheeks burned with color and she worked the candy furiously, her mouth puckering like a fish.

He crunched the sweet lozenge between his molars. "I knew you weren't into it, so I pulled out."

"But..."

"But what? I'll tell you. It was too late to stop, but if I'd stayed inside you I would have felt like I was just using you."

"Oh," she said, going still.

"I wasn't—" He swallowed butterscotch shards, hit with a realization—they were both feeling rejected. "It wasn't that I didn't *want* you."

"Oh."

"I figured you'd changed your mind about me."

She looked down at her thumb, rubbing along the edge of the counter. "I did, sort of. I'm sorry—I couldn't help it. At first it was all so lovely and dreamy, but then..."

"You thought 'What the hell am I doing having sex with an ex-con?'"

She sniffed. "Something like that."

He took a chance and gave her a hug. "Okay, okay. I don't blame you."

Her head moved against his chest. He let go even though he wanted to hold on to her until morning.

Her voice came low and fast. "It's just that you're acting so mysteriously. And those men who are after you—" She shuddered. "If I knew what was going on, maybe I could help you. If I knew I could trust you..."

"Mack, I can't explain."

"Right." She shot him a reproachful look and went back to making tea.

He sifted through his options—again. There were very few. "All I can say is that I'm not as bad as you think. I've been in some trouble, but right now I'm trying to stay—no, get *out* of it."

"Who are the two men who came to my door? Why did they pretend to be police? And why are they after you?"

He chose the easiest to answer. "They called themselves cops because it's the fastest way to get information. Stupid, too, when impersonating an officer is added to their charges. But those kind of guys never think they're going to get caught."

"Those kind? You're not one of them?"

"Not really."

"Because you *have* been to prison?"

He shrugged. Let her think that.

"You didn't say who they are," she remembered.

"Because you can't know."

"And why they're after you..."

"I double-crossed them."

Her eyes widened.

"They found out something was fishy and beat me up," he said, feeding her the surface truth. He touched his ribs. "It would have gotten a lot worse, but I managed to get away. That was when I came here. Last resort. If they'd caught me, I'd be dead right now. Guaranteed."

She shuddered. "Then why don't you just give them what they want and be done with it?"

"What makes you think they want something?" Had she been paying closer attention than she knew? Any knowledge at all put her in jeopardy. She was already there, of course, but on the periphery at this point. It appeared that Sloss and Bonny hadn't figured out that she was involved, so she was relatively safe.

Until he'd crept into her bedroom.

He had no willpower when it came to Mackenzie, and that made her a very dangerous Achilles' heel.

# 7

NEITHER ONE OF THEM was ready to go back to bed since they were ignoring the entire problem of whether or not they were going to do it together, so Mackenzie wasn't surprised when Devlin followed her into the living room. She'd shut off the kitchen light, and for a brief moment the darkness was blessedly comforting. Until she thought of how she'd let herself believe that making love to Devlin in the middle of the night would render her blameless. Then she couldn't get the lamp on fast enough.

She curled up in her familiar chair. Sipped the hot tea. Avoided Devlin's eyes.

He'd been blunt. While talking about how she'd frozen up had rattled her, she was glad they had. Devlin's thoughtfulness was a nice surprise. She hadn't always been superresponsive in her love life with Jason, and he'd never known the difference. A few times, he'd say, "Was it good for you, babe?" as he rolled off her, but even if she didn't answer he never noticed. That Devlin had been so attuned to her, and so caring, was really kind of miraculous.

She'd been sure he was disappointed in her.

If she could be so wrong about that...what about the rest of it?

He'd pretty much admitted to being a thief. It was possible that he was trying to reform. Either way, she believed he was in danger and that was enough for her. She'd let him stay as long as he needed.

But that didn't mean she was ready to trust him with her grandmother's engagement ring.

Or her heart.

Maybe her body...if she could ever learn to separate the two.

Devlin coughed to break the silence. He shifted a leg onto the couch where he'd sprawled out. "Thanks for being my friend."

Her brows arched into a question.

"In case I never said that."

"You mean, back in high school?"

"Then and now. You're a remarkably kind and generous person, Mack."

"My friends think I'm too easygoing. Sedate to the point of being dormant. I guess I was, but thank heaven for Sabrina. I had been *thinking* of making changes in my life. She was the one who pushed me into actually following through."

"The haircut?"

She smiled. "Why are you so stuck on my hair?"

"Because in my head I always pictured you with long hair."

He pictured her in his head? *Always?*

"Yeah," he said, clearly reading her face. "I've thought of you a lot over the years."

She swallowed. Had she been so caught up in nursing her crush on Devlin that she'd missed the signs that he might feel a little something for her? Amazing.

And did that mean that Devlin had been making love to her, not just having sex with a warm and convenient body?

"I had no idea," she said. "You treated me like a kid sister when we were in school together. I was tolerable, useful, someone you were fond of...."

"You were more than that."

"I'm not sure that I can believe you."

"Because I never told you?" He leaned forward, one elbow resting on his thigh, trying to make her look at him. "Because I never kissed you?"

"Yes," she whispered, staring at the mug balanced on her knee.

"Mack, you were out of my league. I wasn't even going to try."

"What?" she squawked. "You could have had any girl you wanted. Including me!"

"I knew that. But I was smarter than you—in that one way."

"I don't understand."

"You might have been temporarily intrigued by me, but we wouldn't have lasted as a couple. You were going on to college. I was going nowhere."

"No, Devlin—you were smart enough. You could have gone to college if you'd tried." But she remembered how he'd disliked classrooms, how he'd disdained autocratic teachers, arbitrary rules, the social killing fields of teenage peer pressure. He'd ignored all of it and did as he pleased. That was why he'd been so cool.

"What about your parents? What would they have said if you'd started dating me?"

She shrugged. "Who cares?"

"You know you would have."

She knew that if Devlin had showed any interest, he was the one thing she'd have rebelled about. After the divorce, which had come when she was twelve, she'd always been conscious of not creating any further problems for her parents, particularly her mother. She'd become even more meticulous and restrained, filling the role of the good daughter that Sabrina had scorned.

Mackenzie met Devlin's eyes. "You never gave me a chance. I might have surprised you."

Fascination etched his face. "You surprise me now."

"I surprise myself."

"Is there a chance for us, do you think?"

Her heart was pounding in her throat, it seemed. "There might be."

"What would I have to do to make that happen?"

"Go straight."

He sighed. Looked away. "Damn, I knew you'd say that."

"You won't even try?"

"It's more complicated than that."

"You're *making* it complicated."

They were back in the same place where they'd started. Except now she'd tasted what making love with Devlin was like. She'd glimpsed his good character and the emotions he was careful not to show. And she wanted him all the more for it.

ON THE SURFACE, nothing much happened for the next couple of days. Mackenzie and a disguised Devlin left her apartment as before, but there was no further sign of the men he'd cheated. He escorted her to Sweet Something without incident. She always invited him in, but he'd say he had things to do and then vanish into the city. She had no idea where he went or what he did—and whether it was illegal or not. In the middle of the night, he'd come back, stealing in the back door, once in the disguise but otherwise not. She always awakened, but they didn't exchange a word. After that one time, Devlin went straight to the couch without stopping.

*That* night, when she'd finally finished her tea and got up to go to bed, he'd said, with such a careless air that she could do nothing but agree, "I'll sleep out here." Ever since, she wished she'd answered differently.

On the third day, Devlin showed up unexpectedly at Sweet Something, a couple of hours before closing time. He was in the disguise, although somewhere along the way he'd substituted a plain blue T-shirt for the sparkly one. Mackenzie's employees gawked when she brought him over to the candy counter for introductions.

"Jeff, Lena, LaShaundra, this is my friend, Dev—"

"Elton," Devlin said, giving her a discreet nudge.

She swallowed the rest of his name.

"Elton Devine." He aimed an uncharacteristic toothy smile at the goggling employees. "I work with Blair. Have you met Blair? Or should I say Goddess Galorious?"

They nodded and murmured, getting it now, although LaShaundra measured his chest with her eyes and said, "I'm guessin' you don't wear strapless gowns, Elton."

He shrugged. "I'm new. They usually stick me in the back row of the chorus line."

Mackenzie grabbed his arm. "Want the tour?" As they turned, she added, "Thought I'd better get you out of there before Lena was offering makeup tips, and LaShaundra was advising you to up your hormone dosage."

Devlin looked back at the male employee in an apron with hot pink stripes. "What about Jeff?"

"Jeff is working his way through college. He's a voice major, so he might offer to check your pitch on 'It's Raining Men' if you don't look out."

Devlin winked at her, his orange-blond hair shining under the pendant lights. "Hallelujah."

She smiled and swept an arm in the air. "Well, this is my store."

"Incredible place." Devlin looked all around at the

glass and shiny chrome and rainbow of neon colors. A number of customers were lined up at the candy counter. Others strolled around the store, exclaiming over the artistic displays of familiar old-time candies, or settled at the tables and chairs with soft drinks and bags of candy purchased by the scoop.

"I'm surprised," he said.

"Surprised?"

"When you said you had a penny-candy store, I pictured an old-fashioned place. Small and crowded, like a general store. This is the opposite."

"The presentation's the thing in Manhattan," she explained. "I had to make coming to this store an experience. There's not a lot of margin in the hard candy business, so I concentrated on flash, volume and tourists. We also have a Web site and a catalog in the works for mail-order sales."

"Aren't the same candies available in every corner store?"

"Only some of them. Others are rare, vintage brands. I did a lot of research to track down obscure companies. In a few instances, I was able to persuade them to do a special run for me alone by placing an extra large order."

"Your success is impressive."

"Thank you." Mackenzie walked over to a steel bulkhead made up of a row of candy bins with fish-eye portholes. Each one was lit from within, illuminating heaps of candy. Orange, lime and pink plastic tubes twisted into spirals and angles around the futuristic gum ball machines. "Do you have a quarter?"

Devlin reached into his pocket. He was carrying a ruby worth at least a hundred grand, but he had to dig for spare change. The past few days, he'd been working his informants, hoping to wrap up the case against the Fat Man before Sloss and Bonny ran him down. He'd been skulking in dive bars and back rooms, hiding his weird hair under a do-rag, always keeping one eye on the door. Every moment of exposure had been a risk. His only relief was having Mackenzie's place to go back home to at night.

He also returned to Mackenzie, even though all he'd seen of her was her wide-open eyes gleaming at him in the dark bedroom, and a half hour of small talk over coffee and English muffins or bagels in the morning.

A comfort, all the same.

He held up the quarter, but she told him to choose. He looked over the displays and fed the coin into a slot. When he cranked the handle, the gum ball machine didn't drop a candy with a tame little plop. It shot the tiny pack of Smarties through the twisted tubes.

"Pneumatic," Mackenzie said. She slid open a tiny window and he took out his candy. She smiled. "So you're a Smarties boy."

"I prefer kisses that taste like butterscotch."

Her smile was shy, but her eyes shined with daring.

She tapped the porthole filled with the golden glow of her favorite candy. "Got another quarter?"

He kissed her instead. A quick peck, but appetizing. "A little sweet something," he said in a low voice for her alone.

Pleasure flashed across her face. "That's what my mom always used to say when she broke a diet. 'Girls, I need a little sweet something.' It was the perfect name for my store."

"And for you."

"Sweet talker." She gave him a gentle push. "You're going to blow your cover."

"What's upstairs?" he said, checking out the balcony. The store wasn't large, but the open second story gave it an airy feeling.

"I'll show you." Mackenzie led him to a spiral staircase set among a group of tall columns that soared all the way up to the balcony. Each column was made of clear Plexiglas and filled with candy. Gum balls and lollipops, but primarily jawbreakers in various sizes and colors. Green, orange, pink, yellow, red.

*Red*, he thought, eying the candy as he climbed the stairs. *No, that was a crazy idea.*

*So crazy it might work.*

"What are these supposed to be?" he asked Mackenzie. They'd reached the second floor and he leaned over the railing, examining the upper reaches of one of the candy columns. There was a good-sized hatch door built into the top surface.

. "Grandiosity." Mackenzie laughed. "Sabrina says I have a Willie Wonka complex."

"I'm surprised your employees aren't dressed like Oompa-Loompas."

"I tried, but they objected to the padding and face paint."

Devlin slid a hand across the hatch. "This is for re-filling?"

"Yes, although I don't expect the columns to be running low anytime soon. Think of them as decorative storage. Like a corn silo for jawbreakers."

He straightened. "Interesting."

The ruby was burning a hole in the toe of his boot. He'd carried it there for the past few days, ever since Bonaventure had caught him going through the goods from the safe in the back room of Fat's Yonkers pawn-shop. He'd only been trying to identify various pieces as hot—the ruby was identifiable even though it had been taken from its setting—but Bonny had accused Devlin of stealing. While the lower-level thug was busy calling Sloss for instructions, Devlin had managed to slip the ruby inside his boot. Sloss had arrived and at Fat Man's command they'd transported Devlin to a waterfront warehouse for "interrogation." Fortunately, their pat-down had been a cursory search for weapons. Only later was the ruby—and then Devlin—missed.

He'd been playing it very carefully since then, working his informants to tighten the noose on the Fat Man and his henchmen. The hot ruby was crucial evidence, but Devlin had been too hot himself to make contact with Jakes and turn it in. He'd thought of hiding it in Mackenzie's apartment, but that had seemed too dangerous. Sloss and Bonny could still show up there.

No one would expect felonious doings at a wacky wonderland like Sweet Something.

"My office is this way," Mackenzie said.

Devlin followed her, hovering in the doorway. The room was simply furnished in dark wood and gray walls. "It's...nice."

She wrinkled her nose. "It doesn't suit the rest of the store, does it? I thought I should have one room that looked normal, but that was a mistake. The designer's plan was for fake fur carpets and mirrored walls and I got a little worried about how I'd ever work in a room like that."

"I couldn't work in any kind of an office at all."

Her head cocked. "Have you ever tried?"

"Not really." Out of high school, he'd tried various dead-end jobs. Before long he'd seen the wisdom of Don Richards's advice and soon after he'd gotten serious about a career in law enforcement, filling time with night-school classes until he was accepted into the police academy. Postgraduation, he'd gone almost directly into undercover work. He had the look and the kind of shady background that could be expanded into his street identity— "Devil" Brandt. No one in his previous life had trouble believing his cover story of the escalating misdeeds that had resulted in a year in prison. Although his parents knew the truth, they were sworn to keep the secret. That was tough on them. Especially his mother, who ranted frantically in her "up" phases and suffered in martyred silence when she was down. His father was simply relieved his son had been saved from a life of crime.

Mackenzie put on a stern expression. "You need to find a real job, Devlin."

"Yes, ma'am."

"Have you thought of contacting the police?"

His brows went up. "For a job?"

"Ha! No, to report whatever's going on with you."

"There's no need. I can take care of myself."

"Right." She snorted. "I see the scrapes are almost healed. How about the ribs?"

"No problem." He put his hands on his waist and flexed for her. Her gaze lingered and he thought she was admiring him until he remembered he was wearing Elton John glasses and Greg Brady pants.

Mackenzie's voice dropped. "What if I call the police myself?"

"Why would you do that?"

"Because I'm worried about you and I think you need protection." She went on hurriedly. "Besides, you can't hide out at my place forever. Eventually…"

"I'm taking care of it."

"That's where you are, 'taking care of it' until two in the morning?"

"I've been waking you. Sorry." He was only sorry that she'd made no overture toward inviting him back into her bed. After the first time had ended badly, he'd promised himself that he wouldn't make the same mistake twice. Whether that meant not sleeping with her, or making sure to finish properly the next time, he wasn't quite sure. The latter, he suspected. His willpower was weak where she was concerned.

"It's not that, Devlin. I worry about you."

"Nothing will happen to me. And I promise I'll be out of your life soon enough."

She lifted her face to his, her nostrils flaring and her eyes burning like coals. He remembered her having the same expression when she was sixteen, those rare times when she'd had enough of playing the doormat and had stood up for herself. Sometimes with a classmate or her sister, sometimes with him. He'd once shown up outside her bedroom at midnight to ask her to type his term paper due the next day—which meant to revise and correct it as well. She'd given him the same look right before she slammed the window.

"If you think that's what I want," she said angrily, "you haven't been paying attention."

"I'm paying attention. Why do you think I'm still here?"

Her eyes widened. "Tell me."

"Because—"

The phone rang. She ignored it.

"Go ahead and answer it," he said. "After you're done I'll take you out for dinner and we can discuss all the ways I can demonstrate my interest in you."

"A real dinner? In public?"

He grinned, something he'd been doing more of since their reunion. "Answer the phone."

Shaking her head, she reached for the receiver.

He eased back out of her office to the balcony area. The employees were closing shop, ushering out the final customers, clearing the tables. They weren't looking up.

He knelt and untied his boot, fishing inside for the ruby. It had to be from the set of the matching necklace and ring stolen on Park Avenue a week ago. When it was matched by experts, he'd finally have proof that Boris Cheney was up to his double chins in the active fencing of stolen goods.

Mackenzie was still talking on the phone. He reached over the railing and opened the hatch on the column that was filled with red jawbreakers.

"Devlin?"

He froze, the ruby clenched in his fist.

"I'll be ready to go in two seconds," Mackenzie called from the office.

Quickly he thrust his arm into the clear column, digging deeply into the jawbreakers so the ruby wouldn't be too close to the top. He'd noticed the scoops and coin slots at the base of the columns, so he knew the candy was sold from the bottom first. The ruby would be safely concealed among the jawbreakers for some time to come.

He was pulling on his boot when Mackenzie came out of the office carrying a briefcase. She gave him a curious look. "Pebble in your shoe?"

"Wrinkle in my sock," he said.

"Isn't it too hot for boots?"

"Probably."

"You're a very odd man, Devlin Brandt. I can't figure you out."

"Hey, up there!" one of the girl employees called. "Mackenzie, do you mind if we play the jukebox while we clean up?"

Mackenzie looked over the railing. "Sure."

"Come down and join us."

Mackenzie looked at Devlin and said, "Want to?" as "On the Good Ship Lollipop" started playing.

He listened. "That's a familiar song, but it's not Shirley Temple."

"A version by Rudy Vallee. I'm surprised Lena picked it—she usually prefers the song about cotton candy by the Insane Clown Posse." She explained as they wound down the spiral stairs. "I had the jukebox stocked with candy songs. Never let it be said I don't know how to wring every grain of sugar out of a theme."

The kids were bopping to the music as they wiped down tables and pushed brooms across the floor. Devlin looked at the play list. "'Candy Man' by Sammy Davis, Jr. Okay, that's a given. But we also have a 'Candy Boy' and 'Candy Girl'...and here's 'Sugar Walls.' Sheena Easton?" He laughed. "Plus three songs called 'Candy' by Will Smith, Mandy Moore and Foxy Brown. Quite a variety of artists."

Mackenzie was opening her purse and pumping

quarters into the jukebox. "I prefer the upbeat songs."
She punched the numbers for "Sugar, Sugar" by the
Archies and "Lollipop" by the Chordettes.

"Is that an invitation to dance?"

"Well, I—" She seemed flustered.

He looked at the employees, who were flailing arms
and swinging hips. Jeff was singing into the handle of
his push broom as if it were a microphone. "I think we
have to dance."

Devlin took Mackenzie's hand. He didn't know
how to jitterbug or swing, but he could mirror a few of
Jeff's moves. As they danced, he loosened up, watching Mackenzie's laughing face as she swiveled, shimmied, snapped her fingers and shook her rump. The
music was infectious.

"We've never danced before," she said at one point,
flushed and out of breath.

"Not at a high-school dance?"

"I don't remember you going to any."

"I was probably out in the parking lot smoking
weed."

"I'd hoped you'd ask me to prom," she said as he
attempted an awkward spin. She made it work, twirl-
ing away from him.

He grabbed her hand again and spun her back into
his arms. "I had no idea."

Her eyes sparkled as she laughed up into his face.
"You were clueless about me!"

*She was right*, he thought, stopping and watching
her dance away. *He'd been clueless in a moronic teenage-*

*male way, going for the girls whose beauty was skin-deep instead of deep-hearted.* He valued Mackenzie so much more now.

She was looking particularly fetching with color in her cheeks and her full lips curved into a happy smile. Her skirt wasn't short, but it was tight, hugging her bottom as she waggled it back and forth to a song with the refrain, "I want candy."

Soon they were all singing it, hopping up and down and waving their arms overhead as if they were at a rock concert. *"I want candy!"*

Devlin stepped behind Mackenzie, sliding his hands over her upraised arms so they lowered and his arms crisscrossed around her. He waited for the next refrain, driven wild by the swish of her hips against his groin, and then whispered into her ear. "I want Mackenzie."

She stiffened. They were in sync, there.

She opened her mouth, but no voice emerged. The song faded out. The dancing stopped. LaShaundra dropped into a chair, mopping her face with a sleeve.

"Party's over," Mackenzie said. Devlin guessed he was the only one who heard the wobble, although Lena was looking at them with an alert expression. He moved his hands to Mackenzie's shoulders, hoping that looked more appropriate.

In high spirits, the three employees finished up and departed as a group, waving and calling goodbyes. Devlin could see that Mackenzie was a well-liked boss, but that was no surprise. She probably let them sample all the free candy they could eat.

She moved away from him. "So...dinner?"

"After one more song." He returned to the jukebox.

"Not 'Sugar Walls' or 'Sex and Candy,'" she said.

"Okay," he agreed, finding another that would do.

She looked relieved until the music started and he walked toward her...slowly, with dangerous intent. He'd selected "Pour Some Sugar on Me" by Def Leppard.

"I should be, ah, closing up," she said, but her halting words didn't seem to match the movements of her lips. Maybe because he was only looking, not listening.

He was nearly upon her. She ducked away. "Let me lock the door."

"Good idea."

She darted to the door and slid the bolts.

"And turn off the lights," he said, soft and suggestive, although he'd realized that with the glass storefront they were on display to anyone walking or driving by. Enough days had passed that there was almost no chance that he'd be tracked to an upscale candy emporium in the Village, but...

The store went dark.

"Pour some sugar on me," wailed the singer.

Devlin went to Mackenzie and lifted her arms to his shoulders. He put his hands on her waist. She let out a soft moan and moved up against him, her hips moving back and forth with a slow, sexy rhythm of their own. The music throbbed, seeming to grow louder as they teased each other, bodies grazing for a few tantalizing seconds before swaying apart and then coming together again with a sweet, provocative pressure.

Desire pulsed in the air. His blood roared with it. Mackenzie was made up of a hundred enticing curves, from her bare legs and the hint of cleavage revealed by the open collar of her blouse to the softness of her arms, curling around his head and shoulders in a warm embrace. Her dark eyes were wide open and welcoming, pinned to his as they danced.

*Wide awake,* he thought. This time, she knew what she was doing.

"Are you—" he put his mouth to her ear and echoed the singer "—hot sticky sweet?"

She shuddered against him, making a rough-edged purring sound that wasn't an answer, only an invitation.

His hands lowered to her bottom. She moved her rounded thighs against him, and he was so engaged by the thought of being cradled between them that he let go, forgetting where they were and why she shouldn't have anything to do with him. All he knew was a hard, driving hunger.

"I can't wait to find out," he said, sliding his mouth across her cheek until his forehead was pressed to hers.

Her tongue flicked across his lips. "I'm ready."

# 8

"THAT'S NOT DEVIL," Bonny said. "Look at the way he's dressed, like a chick. Look at the clown hair."

"You're an idiot."

"I'm telling you—"

"Shut your damn trap and let me think." Arthur Sloss squinted past the windshield, watching as the cab pulled away. Devil wasted no time in getting the woman inside. Sloss remembered her. First apartment, ground floor, next door to the cross-dressing freak. New York City had gone to hell in a handbasket when even the normal-looking ones like Devil's squeeze were into the weird stuff.

Sloss looked again at the wrinkled, stained reunion booklet. He'd picked it up the night they'd been stuck hunting for Devil in the rain, had glanced through it without noticing any significance, and tossed it to the floor of the car. This morning he'd flipped through it after he'd peeled it off his shoe. And there had been the double-crossing punk himself, in black-and-white. High school. Named *Devlin* Brandt, but Devil was just a dumb nickname anyway. There was no other information, except that Sloss had remembered where he'd found the booklet. They'd been waiting outside the apartment since noon and he'd grown more insulted by the minute. That plump girl from 1A had *lied* to him. He'd known the wet scarf was suspicious, but she'd looked so honest he'd let it go.

"Is Devil one of them transvestites?" Bonny was busy straightening the pleats in his trousers. No Freudian meaning there. "We shared the john. The perv musta been checking me out."

"It's a disguise, moron." But Sloss wasn't positive. Brandt had a reason for choosing this particular skirt's apartment—they were connected somehow. Had to be more than old time's sake. As for the cutesy clothes...

Sloss grimaced. Hell, those two were probably getting it on right this very minute.

They watched the window, but no light went on. Didn't freaks like to *see* each other, all dressed as they were?

Bonny shot his cuffs. "Can I go get him now?"

Sloss sneered at his partner. The kid was big and strong, but a little too eager. "We're waiting. Fat Man wants the ruby back first. Then you can do whatever you want." *Freak. They were all freaks. Not like the good old days when there was honor among thieves.*

"I'M MAKING NO PROMISES, Mackenzie."

"I know that. Don't worry. I am *not* made of sugar. I might cry a little when you leave me, but I won't melt."

Devlin brushed his knuckles across her cheek, the

look in his eyes as soft as his touch. "I don't want to make you cry, either."

"Then stay with me." She moved into his arms and said, "Please," even though she'd sworn to herself that she wouldn't beg. She wanted to take this for what it was and not fall into the trap of trying to fix his life for him. Devlin was his own man.

Not her man.

Except for tonight.

"Patience," he said, nuzzling her neck. "You never know how things will work out." He lipped her lobe, his breath warm and tingly on the inside of her ear. "Okay?"

She held back from asking what he meant. *Don't cling, don't plead, don't nag,* she told herself. *Remember, you're blissfully single and as in control of your sexuality as you are of your career.*

She threaded her fingers through Devlin's hair. "Okay."

They lowered to the couch, arms and legs already tangled. He'd been ready to make love at Sweet Something, up in her office, but she'd hesitated. Part of her had wanted to prove she was up for adventurous sex, but she'd known she'd be a lot more comfortable at home. Since this might be her last chance with Devlin, she wanted this time to be good—even unforgettably spectacular—for both of them. Devlin had been a shade resistant about going in her front door, apparently still worrying over maintaining his cover, but she'd pointed out that his disguise was in place and then started kissing him in the back of the cab. Soon he'd stopped thinking about anything but getting her inside the apartment as fast as he could, whether or not they were watched.

Now Devlin was kissing her and fumbling with her buttons. She let him finish, then slipped out of the blouse, but covered his hands when they went to the front clasp of her bra. "Patience," she said with a teasing smile. "You gave me instructions earlier."

He stroked and squeezed her through the satin cups until her nipples were as hard as pebbles. "Instructions? I don't remember any instructions."

"Wait here." She kicked off her shoes and ran into the kitchen, not bothering with the lights except for the small one that was always lit over the stove. She flung open a cupboard, grabbed a Sweet Something goody bag—how fortunate that she was always stocked for candy emergencies—and hurried back to Devlin before self-consciousness could catch up to her.

He was lounging on the couch, his arms crossed behind his head. No glasses, boots or wrinkled socks. The T-shirt and fanny pad were gone. So was the bandage around his ribs. He still wore the silly striped pants, hiked so short half his hairy calves showed, but that didn't detract from his virility at all. The impressive bulge of his arousal made her stop and swallow, in fact.

Devlin didn't seem to mind the delay. He was smiling as he looked at her, until suddenly she remembered she was half-naked herself and standing before him with a bag of candy. He was probably wondering if she planned to gorge on sugar or on him.

*Well, both,* she thought, feeling bolder as she settled on a cushion, kneeling so she faced him.

"You said..." she opened the cellophane bag of assorted candies, selected a couple of paper straws, and tossed the rest on the coffee table "...pour some sugar on me."

He started to rise, but she put her hand on the center of his chest and made him lie back. She nipped off the tip of the straw, held it above his chest and tipped it at an angle. A thin stream of colored sugar spilled out, the granules scattering over Devlin's bare chest. She tapped the straw with her finger, pouring the remaining sugar lower, over the ridged slab of his stomach.

"Don't move," she said. Most of the purple sugar had made a straight line down his chest, following the natural crease of his muscular physique. Tiny grains had scattered elsewhere however, and she realized that she should have licked him first. That's how she'd eaten Pixy Stix as a girl—licked her finger so the sugar would stick. Or tilted back her head and swallowed...

She'd try that later. She might not be greatly experienced with sex, but she'd amassed a thousand techniques with candy.

"Now," she said, gazing into Devlin's eyes while her stomach fluttered with a combination of nerves and daring. "I am going to lick you."

His look was scorching. "Good idea. I like it hot sticky sweet, remember?"

She bent over him, rewarded by the way he sucked in his breath. Her tongue flicked once, scooping up a tiny sample of the sugar. Then again, giving him a longer lick. "Mmm, you're so sweet."

She lifted a leg and lowered herself into a more intimate position atop his thighs. His erection rubbed against her belly as she ducked toward his chest again, this time starting near his navel and slurping her tongue all the way up to the patch of curly brown hair that covered his pecs. She nuzzled there, searching for traces of sugar, inhaling the manly fragrance of his skin.

Devlin's hands gripped her thighs and she realized that her skirt was so tight it had rolled up to her hips when she'd spread her legs to straddle him. His fingers were pressing into her flesh, stroking closer to the inside of her thighs. Heat blossomed between them.

"Can I taste?" Devlin caught her mouth, sliding his tongue around hers in a delicious, slippery dance.

"Do you like it?" she gasped in between kisses. His hands were on her rump now, and she was flattened upon his chest, rocking against him and then with him as the hollow ache inside her became a fiercely beautiful thing.

"All I taste is you." He didn't sound disappointed. "But let me give it a try."

Her breasts, pushed together by the satin bra so her cleavage was even deeper than usual, were sitting on his chest as if it was a shelf. He cracked one of the sugar-filled straws in half, spilling the contents into the crevice, then grabbed another straw and emptied that on her, too, as she pushed up, laughing at the mess.

"Wait! Stop!" she protested. "I'm going to get roaches."

"In your bra?"

She laughed, loving the way his eyes glittered and his grin twitched so naughtily.

"I'll keep my tongue on you until I've found every grain," he said, pulling her toward him. "I'll lick every inch of your breasts, suck them until—ahh." His tongue dipped into her cleavage, then plunged deep. "Can't get it all." He lifted his head, the tip of his nose sprinkled with the purple sugar. "I'm afraid there's no getting around it. You'll have to take the bra off."

She blinked. "No, *you'll* have to—"

He didn't let her finish. One tug and he'd sprung the hooks. The beige satin bra burst open and her breasts tumbled out, so lavishly round and prominently aroused—her nipples looked like bright pink thimbles—that it was almost embarrassing. The last time she'd known him, she'd still been in the stage where she'd clutched her schoolbooks to her chest so the boys wouldn't make comments about her "girls." Now she was topless and riding Devlin's thighs, getting intimately familiar with his arousal, and strangely enough he seemed to prefer the new her. The brand-new, fabulous her.

Forget the outcome of her bet with Sabrina. Forget the uncertainty of how long Devlin would be around. Mackenzie knew she had won in a way that would stay with her forever.

She dropped her chin and leaned forward, lifting and feeding one breast into Devlin's mouth. He let out a soft moan and did a flickering motion with his tongue, then gave her nipple a wet lick and drew it into a deep warmth, his lips opening as he sucked.

The stimulation was intense. She arched, pressing her belly against his, grinding her hips, lost in the pleasure and heat but knowing that she wasn't lost in a dream.

This was *real*.

MINUTES LATER—maybe longer—Devlin stood, swayed on his feet until the world stopped spinning, then helped Mackenzie up. Her face was flushed, her smile was wide, her breasts were...*wow*. He stopped there and made himself look at the ceiling. He counted to ten, waiting for his blood to cool, or at least drop below the boiling point.

Okay, so that wasn't going to happen. He took Mackenzie's hand and they staggered together through the dark hallway and into the bedroom. "Lights on or off?" he asked, finding the zipper of her skirt without the benefit of sight.

She shimmied her hips so it dropped to her ankles. "On," she said, smiling a private smile as she stepped out of the skirt and walked to the bedside table. "I want to see you." He blinked in surprise and then she switched on the lamp. She turned toward him, sliding a hand across her breasts in a lingering gesture that was halfway shy but completely erotic. Her skin was a rosy pink in the light, and he wondered if she knew how beautiful and lush and desirably female she looked.

He tried to tell her, but his tongue was thick and he didn't know if he was using the right words. She merely smiled, extending her hand, motioning him over. He went to stand in front of her as she tickle-traced her fingernails over his chest, then slowly sank onto the bed. She reached the snap waistband of the striped pants and with a bemused expression popped it open. The inside of her wrist rubbed over his erection. He was twitching, already swollen hard enough to bust right through the zipper if she didn't get it down damn fast.

She took far too long. The torture was incredible, but the release was even better. Especially when she slid her thumb across the head of his shaft and then gave it a lick. Every bone and muscle in his body turned to hot jelly.

"I have an idea," she said, reaching toward the table. For a condom, he thought, until he heard a soft clicking sound. He focused dazedly and there, under the lamp, was a small glass dish of hard candy.

"What—"

She held up a couple of round balls swirled with varied colors. "Jawbreaker sex."

"*What?*"

She laughed. Clearly, either his stupefaction or his state of extreme, impatient arousal was funny.

"The sugar was enough," he said. "Besides, I've never heard of jawbreaker sex and I'm not sure I want to."

"Don't you dare?" Teasingly, she rolled the jaw-breakers along his abdomen beneath her flattened palm.

He put a finger beneath her chin and tilted her face up. "What's involved? No actual breaking of the jaw?" Although...

She kept up the rolling massage. Smiling and rolling and— *oh, man!*—reaching for his bobbing erection. "Bear with me. I'm making this up as I go along." She cocked her head, considering his turgid state and the slippery candies. "Hmm. This might be easier if you got on the bed."

He didn't lie down; he collapsed.

Mackenzie popped a jawbreaker into her mouth.

"Hot damn..." he breathed.

She went on all fours like a cat, rubbing her face against his skin. He was burning with anticipation by the time she reached his lower half, her cheeks hollowing as she sucked on the jawbreaker. Her puckered lips pressed to the head of his erection and then opened, drawing him into the wet heat of her mouth. With her tongue, she rolled the round candy against his shaft, up and down, all around, manipulating him and the candy and then him again until he was shaking. The urge to thrust was unbearable, but despite her natural talent she was a novice, and he didn't want to choke her. How could they explain to the EMTs?

He unclenched his body and reached for her. "Enough with the jawbreaker. I want *you.*"

He dragged her on top. She inserted two fingers into her mouth and removed the shiny jawbreaker, dropping it on the bedside table. "Now what?" he groaned when she rummaged inside the drawer.

She pulled out a strip of condoms. "I bought these...after last time. They're, um..."

He squinted at the colorful packets. "Don't tell me. Flavored."

"We have grape, we have cherry, we have peppermint. Oh, look—it's striped."

"I'd look like a candy cane."

"You wore the striped pants well."

*Candy condoms.* He couldn't believe it. He was supposed to be a tough guy. "Why didn't you get edible undies instead?"

"I'd forgotten that you have such a taste for sugar."

"Sugar on *you,*" he said, emphasizing the *you* again in hopes that she'd get the hint. He couldn't hold off much longer. He had to get inside her.

She moved against him until his arousal was nestled in the cleft between her thighs. "Yeah, and now I'm all hot sticky sweet with wanting you."

He felt it. She was so juicy she oozed. All his blood had rushed south for the duration, leaving him light-headed. He let his head drop onto the pillow. "Okay, I give up. Just pick one. You're the candy expert."

"Well..." She smiled at him while she ran her hand along his flank. "Maybe the candy *sexpert*."

His eyes narrowed. "Do you have butterscotch?"

"Mmm. My favorite flavor."

"Quick," he said, "I'm getting my second wind. It must be a sugar rush."

She opened the packet, he plucked out the condom and together they rolled it on, sheathing him in golden latex. He thought he looked absurd, but the sight of his butterscotched penis made Mackenzie giggle and her enjoyment was most important. Even the silly banter was manageable if it kept her happy. The one thing he wasn't going to give her was a taste of the flavored condom. He'd had too much teasing already.

He kissed her, slowly easing them to a horizontal position. She abruptly stopped laughing and that was good, too. Very good, he saw when he pulled his head back. Her face was glowing—really, truly glowing. "You're beautiful," he said. "The most beautiful woman in the world." He put a hand on her thigh, shifting it to the other side of his body so he fit between her legs. "So beautiful I have to watch you." She lifted up, bracing herself. "Go ahead," he urged. "Sit up. I want to see you."

She bit her lip momentarily, but then eased herself on top of him. "Like this?" she said. He didn't have to answer. She knew what she was doing, taking hold, rising to her knees and then sinking onto him with an excruciating slowness. Finally he was enveloped in her sweet slippery warmth, and the need that rose up, swelling until it filled him, wasn't about the sway of her breasts or the erotic sight of their joining. It was about loving her, loving Mackenzie Bliss—his sweet, shy Mack—the girl he couldn't have and all the woman he'd ever want.

"WAS IT GOOD FOR YOU?"

Mackenzie barely had her breath back. She'd exploded like a firecracker, and if he couldn't tell that her climax had been fantastically powerful, utterly light-my-fuse spectacular...

She looked at his face, one pillow over. "That's a joke, right?"

He was smiling.

She slapped his chest with a lazy hand. "I wouldn't be so smug, Mr. Elton Devine. I have tons of blackmail material on you. Would you want your ex-con pals to know you wear drag queen clothes and butterscotch condoms, huh?"

He'd sobered. "I know you're kidding, Mack, but please be aware that you can't speak to anyone about me. Ever."

He sounded so serious she squeaked in response. "*Anyone?*"

"No one, nowhere, no time. It's important."

"What about my sister?" It was a lucky thing that Sabrina had been so busy with Kit and her job. Now that they were living in the same city, the sisters had become very close again. Sabrina had told Mackenzie everything about Kit, from his first kiss to how she'd finally succumbed to his seduction by chocolate.

"No one."

"But my employees have met you. And Blair."

Devlin frowned. "The employees should be okay—I was in disguise, such as it is, and they don't know me from Adam. But Blair's too sharp, and on the premises. A loose end. I'll have to speak with her to be sure she keeps her mouth shut."

Mackenzie shivered. He sounded so...terse.

"Wow. Then what are you going to do to keep me quiet—kill me?" Her laugh wasn't nearly casual enough to cover her sudden wariness.

"That's not as far-fetched as it should be."

She sucked in a breath. He didn't—*couldn't*—mean...

"Not me, Mack," he said, reaching for her hand. "Don't you know me better than that?"

"Sure, but there is this, uh, situation of yours. Don't you think it's asking a bit much to expect me to trust you, no matter what?"

He flipped over onto his side, propping his head up on his arm. "Don't you?"

"Trust you?" She swallowed. "I guess I do." She'd left the diamond ring in the apartment, after all, even if it was hidden in a pair of balled-up socks. And she'd gotten naked and sweaty with him—twice. If that wasn't trust, what was?

She searched for the honesty in his eyes. He was too

darn skilled at shutting people out, but every now and then the blinkers lifted. Not this time.

She decided to try again to pry some information out of him. "It's your friends, or rather, your *enemies* who I don't trust."

"Good." He repeated it for emphasis. "*Good.*"

"They haven't come back, so what's troubling you?"

He made a sound in his throat, an uneasy *harrumph.* "You know. The usual. Hindsight."

"Are you trying to tell me that you're sorry you made love to me?"

"Not sorry, just cautious."

She turned that over in her mind, weighing her emotional giddiness against the very odd circumstances of their reunion. "All right, then. I won't tell anyone about you."

"Under no circumstances."

"Yessir."

"Except..."

She waited.

"If you're in danger, you say and do *anything* to keep alive."

Not your usual pillow talk. And it certainly didn't sound promising for their rainbow-colored future. "You think I'll be put in danger if you keep seeing me, don't you?"

"That's why I've been careful. But probably not careful enough."

She fought to withhold her worries and questions,

but one slipped out. "Do you think we'll ever be able to have a normal relationship?"

*Oh damn. She'd gone and asked him a dreaded relationship question!*

Surprisingly, Devlin wasn't put off. He even wrapped his arms around her. "I hope so."

She closed her eyes tight and whispered, "So do I."

His fingertips stroked across her breasts. "Because I have an idea for the male-to-female version of jawbreaker sex that I'd love to try out on you."

She snuggled her rear end into his groin, satisfied well enough by the admission even if he'd had to mitigate it. Devlin hadn't changed much since his teenage years—he was accustomed to going it alone, playing his emotions close to the vest. She wondered what it would take to get him to admit that they just might be falling in love.

# 9

"WHAT ARE YOU going to do today?" Mackenzie said over bowls of healthy muesli cereal that tasted like bits of bark and twigs. Devlin had spooned on sugar, reminding her of their Pixy Stix adventure. Her burgeoning sexuality was asking her to come up with 101 uses for Lemonheads, but her practical side was noting that she had to vacuum the couch before leaving for work.

"Nothing special," Devlin said between crunches.

"I could take you clothes shopping."

"Do you think I don't have clothes?"

"As far as I've seen, no."

"That's only because I can't go to my apartment right now. They know where I live."

"Ah." She eyed him dubiously, not sure she wanted to become accustomed to thinking like a wanted criminal. "Where *do* you live?" For some reason, she hadn't thought of him actually having his own place.

"Just a crappy rented room. You wouldn't want to go there."

*All righty, then.* "I wasn't angling for an invitation."

"Hey," he said in a soft voice.

"How often do you go back to the Scarsdale area?"

she asked, both to keep the conversation going and because she'd remembered a classmate at the reunion saying he'd seen Devlin at a notorious pawnshop. She wondered if that was where he sold his stolen goods. Maybe he'd already taken the ruby there.

He supplied one of his patented nonanswers. "Not often."

She narrowed her eyes, watching him spoon up the muesli. He was looking both better and worse. The bruises and cuts were healing, but the color of his ragged hair was painful. He wore the same faded-to-gray denims—without underwear, apparently, or anything else for that matter—and she swore he'd lost ten pounds. His cheeks were gaunt beneath the stubble and there were circles under his eyes. A suitable look for a ne'er-do-well, but not for Elton Devine.

Or her lover.

"You need a hearty breakfast." She got up from the table and started taking ingredients out of the fridge. Real butter, milk, eggs. But he'd have to make do with heart-smart turkey bacon.

Devlin's eyes followed her movements, betraying a trace of longing for home comforts, even while he said, "That's not necessary."

"We've got to keep your strength up." She glanced over her shoulder and added, in case she was sounding too motherly, "You didn't get a lot of sleep last night."

"And whose fault was that?"

She layered the pseudobacon in a frying pan. "I blame it on the jawbreakers."

The doorbell rang.

Devlin, who'd been lounging with the sports section, straightened up. His face changed. It was difficult for Mackenzie to put her finger on how it changed, but it had as if he'd put on a mask. Maybe she was seeing the jewel thief's standard game face. Always be on guard.

They both went to the door. "Let me look," he said, acting all manly and take-charge.

She stepped aside without argument, absorbed in figuring him out. His actions, his past and his character were at odds. Instead of providing insight, their intimacy was making her more confused than ever. How could he be so tender and loving in the dark, and then—

"It's only Blair," he said, interrupting her thoughts.

Mackenzie let her neighbor in. "You're up early."

"I'm just getting home." Blair entered the apartment, her face lighting up when she saw Devlin hovering in the kitchen doorway. "Hey, sweetcakes. Need a new outfit?"

"You women." Devlin shoved his hands into his pockets, looking like a sexy backcountry scalawag with his whiskers, rumpled hair, bare feet and lanky, beat-up body. "Always trying to dress a guy up."

Blair walked toward him, long legs flashing beneath a red leather miniskirt. "Mmm-mm-mmm. I'd be willing to undress you, but Mackenzie might object."

"Think I'll go take a shower." Devlin excused himself and fled into the bathroom with unseemly haste.

Blair batted her fake lashes at Mackenzie. "Was it something I said?"

"I think you scare him almost as much as you fascinate him."

Blair elevated her voice. "Hon, when they get a load of my package, they're *all* scared…at first."

Mackenzie laughed. "Give it up. I told Devlin you're a woman." She went to rescue the bacon.

Blair followed, checking out the table settings. "Cozy. So you two are, shall we say, involved?" She hooted. "Involved. Such a ladylike way to put it. But definitely something you'd do."

"Looks that way." The short answer made Mackenzie smile to herself. She sounded like Devlin.

"Splendid."

"You mean that?"

Blair opened the refrigerator and took out the orange juice. "If he's making you happy, I'm happy."

"But?"

"What's with the disguise?"

"I've been wondering when you'd get around to asking."

"I was trying to be discreet." Blair tilted her head back and drank from the carton, her long red hair brushing the small of her back. She caught Mackenzie's eye as she came up for air. "Not my forte." Her voice lowered. "Is he into kinky stuff? Play-acting? Whips, chains, sex toys?"

"No!" Did candy condoms count?

"Well, hon, there's something going on with him. Watch your step." Blair looked again at the table. "It's not like you to play house so fast. You didn't have a sleepover with Jason until...when? Six months?"

"Devlin's not Jason."

"But you're still you, even with the makeover."

Mackenzie dropped bread in the toaster. "I'm different with Devlin."

"Or it could be that he's Mr. Right. After all, you've been thinking about him for ten years, so this is hardly a fly-by-night affair."

Mackenzie winced as she scrambled the eggs. *That's exactly what it is.*

As far as Devlin was concerned, perhaps.

"Not for my part," she muttered, ducking her chin.

Blair came closer and leaned over the sink so she could look into Mackenzie's face. "Be careful, girl-friend. You're in love with a man who—" She stopped, straightening. "Hey, Devlin."

The toast and Mackenzie popped up simulta-neously. Instead of getting flaky over the question of whether or not Devlin had overheard that she was *in love* with him, she grabbed the slices of hot toast with her fingers and said, "Ouch, ouch, ouch," as she dropped them onto the counter and then a plate. She stole a look at Devlin, who'd resorted to wearing Blair's glitzy mauve T-shirt. A towel was draped around his neck and his wet hair was definitely getting even more orange, no two ways about it. But he still looked sexy.

And dangerous.

She put on a cheery smile. "Breakfast's ready!"

DEVLIN MADE THEM leave by the back door. There had been no sign of trouble, but he said he was just being cautious so she went along with it. Then he threw her another curve. Instead of vanishing the way he usually did, he agreed to accompany her to Sweet Something. Whether it was out of protectiveness or togetherness, she didn't know and wasn't prepared to ask. Better to enjoy her thief of hearts while she had him.

She put him to work behind the candy counter, giving him an orange-and-white striped apron to match his hair. He fit in amazingly well with her other workers, acting as lighthearted and genial as she'd ever seen him. Even though he'd told her not to mend his life, she began to entertain fantasies of offering him a job, helping him go legit. Changing lives was becoming her specialty, wasn't it?

Look how well she'd done with her own... providing Devlin didn't end up breaking her heart.

She tried to keep to her office upstairs and get some neglected work done. But the store was an attractive nuisance at any time; with Devlin on the premises, she couldn't resist. All afternoon they scooped candy together while LaShaundra handled the cash register and the soda fountain drinks. Lena was in the back, checking inventory and unloading boxes of fresh supplies.

"Enjoying yourself?" Mackenzie asked Devlin at one point.

He was waiting for a couple of teenage girls to make up their mind what flavor of jelly beans they wanted. "You actually call this work?"

"Don't discount the sore feet and blisters." She ripped off a two-foot section of candy dots, measuring the length against her outstretched arm before handing the paper strip to a child who already wore a matching set of candy jewelry. "Scooping jelly beans can cause carpal tunnel syndrome."

"I'll bet." He took the girls' order and shoveled a mix of jalapeño, PB&J and watermelon beans into the drawstring cellophane candy bags printed with the Sweet Something logo.

"I offer medical," she said with a grin. "You have a job. Anytime."

He gave her a look but no answer. It was noon, and suddenly the store was overrun with office workers. Mackenzie called Lena in and they scooped like maniacs for the next hour or so.

When the rush was over, Devlin looked a little less cocky—he'd mistaken Sugar Babies for Sugar Daddies and had found out that was not a good thing when dealing with a sugar addict in need of a fix. Mackenzie said he deserved a break, so she got them two soft drinks and brought him to the back room. They sat on cardboard boxes surrounded by industrial shelves filled with boxed stock. Brand names and bright graphics were stacked to the ceiling.

Music drifted from the front. The jukebox was playing "Candy-O" by the Cars.

Mackenzie thought of how Devlin had given her a big candy "O" the night before.

"You're flushed," he said.

"I told you—it's strenuous work."

He chuckled. "Not so much."

"No, but it is fun, isn't it? I love watching the kids with their hands and noses pressed to the glass like— well, like a kid in a candy store. And it's great when a middle-aged adult comes in and gets all excited because we have the brands they remember from their childhood and haven't seen in years. Candy brings back good memories for a lot of people."

Devlin nodded from his position across from her, leaning against a box stamped Bazooka. "You're a sweet person, Mack."

"I know it's not rocket science or curing cancer. Guess you wouldn't want to wear an apron and scoop candy all your life, huh?"

"I can think of worse businesses to be in."

The smile dropped from her face. "Seems to me that you can give up your, um, line of work anytime you want."

"You're right," he said, unexpectedly. His gaze was distant.

"So?"

"As soon as I make this case."

She frowned. "Make what case?"

He straightened up with a snap. "I meant case this joint—" He stopped again and expelled a snort, clearly disgusted with himself. "Aw, hell. Forget you heard that." His expression was aggrieved. He ran a restless hand through his hair, avoiding her eyes.

She was prickling with an aroused instinct that said there was even more of a mystery about him than she'd first suspected, but she didn't know what to make of the clues—or of him.

He turned away, muttering, "Damn, I'm losing my edge."

"That happens when you come to candyland," she said with a nervous laugh.

Her brain was flying along another track, but the scenery was a blur.

Devlin slammed his soft drink on the surface of a box. "This isn't working for me. I've got to get out of here."

She didn't dare ask.

The train inside her head was slowing. "Make the case" sounded like detective talk. "Case the joint" had obvious criminal intonations. Either Devlin was running a sting or planning a job. Both options were alarming.

He started to leave, then came back and stood in front of her. She lifted her gaze. The jukebox was playing bouncy '50s music, not at all a fitting counterpoint to the charged atmosphere, but she barely heard it.

Devlin took her face between his hands and kissed her with all the sweetness and emotional longing their first harsh kiss had lacked. She covered his hands with her own, wanting desperately to prolong the moment because it felt like goodbye. "I love you," she said as soon as he began to pull back. "And I think you might love me."

"That's another of my mistakes," he said, and strode out of the storage room.

She clenched her fists, gritted her teeth, squeezed her eyes shut. Anything to keep her dread—and crazy, careening hope—under control.

"I'M SKINNED," Jimmy Pickles said when Devlin finally ran the scrawny, aging street punk to ground at the Delancey Street basketball courts. He held out a shaky hand. "See that? Nicotine withdrawal. I need my smokes."

Devlin forked over a twenty. "Buy yourself a sandwich while you're at it." Not likely. Nicotine wasn't Jimmy's only addiction. "You followed the Fat Man?"

"It ain't good news." Jimmy Pickles rubbed his nose. He was called Jimmy Pickles because as a kid his family had lived over a pickle store and the smell had soaked into every piece of clothing he wore. Maybe even into his pores. Although twenty years later he smelled more like stale sweat and cigarettes, Devlin still got a whiff of brine when he stood too close.

"Spare me the build-up. What did you find out?"

Jimmy's left eye twitched. "The man's taking meet-ings."

Devlin swore. Cheney was finally making a move, and here *he* was, out of action, peddling penny candy and letting a woman from a past life fog up his brain.

"Meetings with who?"

"Bunches of people. Big, fat people."

*What?* "Family, you mean?" Boris Cheney was an operation unto himself as far as Devlin knew. That was why it had been so difficult to gather evidence against him—the man talked to no one. Sloss was clos-est to the top, but he and Bonny still did all the dirty work.

Jimmy Pickles scratched his underarm. "My mom needs a new air conditioner. She about died during the hot spell."

"Right." Devlin didn't bother arguing, just handed over another bill. He had less than fifty bucks left. There'd been expenses, like the T-shirt and bandanna he'd bought off a street vendor on the way to the Lower East Side. Elton Devine wouldn't make it out of this neighborhood alive, so he'd layered one shirt over the other and tied the bandanna around his Cream-sicle hair.

Jimmy Pickles was looking at Devlin's arms. He folded them, glaring so the snitch wouldn't ask about the faded henna tattoos. "Jimmy...where were the meetings? Who were the people?"

"I followed Fat Man's car the way you said. Sloss

was driving. They went to the Grand Avenue rec center."

"A rec center? You sure?"

"Yeah, yeah, yeah." Jimmy Pickles bobbed his head. "See, I been there for my twelve-step meetings."

Devlin scanned the courts and surrounding street, his gaze skimming over the normal activity—pickup b-ball games, strutting hoochie mamas, hip-hop booming from one direction, Latin beat from another, and always a pack of screeching children running down the streets. He was taking a risk, standing out in the open like this. But he had to end this case fast, before he put Mackenzie in serious jeopardy. "Tell me."

"I went inside to get a look. Fats was in a meeting with this bunch of big people. Real heifers, some of 'em. Made me crave a jelly donut, just looking in."

"Jimmy, you goof. That was a diet meeting."

"Yeah, yeah, I know. Overeaters Unanimous. You said watch Fat Man. That's what I did."

Devlin counted to ten before he spoke. "Give me back my money." He shot out a hand and grabbed Jimmy Pickles by the collar. "I'm not interested in the man's weight problem."

"Hey! Now, wait. I got more."

"It had better be good."

"Heard it this morning when I went into O'Shaughnessey's for a nip. Hair of the dog, that's all."

"I'm not interested in your liquid diet, either."

"So you know Catskill? The guy the Fat Man ran out of business?"

Devlin let go. "Yeah?"

"Bonny's screwing Catskill's sister, is how this came about. Bonny was bragging to her last night how they tracked you down to some girl's house. They got you, man. They know where you been hiding."

"That can't be." Alarm iced Devlin's gut. "They would have come for me."

Jimmy Pickles shrugged. "All's I know is what I heard—something 'bout a school reunion." He cackled as he backed away. "Glad I'm not in your shoes, man. You're gonna be sorry you ever double-crossed the Fat Man."

MACKENZIE WAS supposed to drop the engagement ring off at Decadence on her way home, but she'd forgotten it in the sock drawer this morning, what between Blair asking questions and ducking out the back way with Devlin. She called Kit at the restaurant, and they'd agreed to meet tomorrow morning instead, which was the day of the intended proposal. Sabrina wouldn't be there; she'd be setting up for the charity luncheon.

Hoping against hope that Devlin would show up, Mackenzie delayed at Sweet Something for as long as seemed reasonable, then fifteen minutes more. Finally, she decided it was too late to walk and as she avoided the subway at night, she took a cab home. Her thoughts remained on Devlin. He might sneak in the back way again, her mysterious midnight lover.

"It was fun at first," she told the cabbie, "but now the thrill is beginning to wear off."

"Always does," he said, giving her a sympathetic glance in the rearview mirror.

She gnawed her lip. It wasn't the sex—that was so new and amazing that she couldn't imagine ever growing tired of it. But the uncertainty...

"Is there something wrong with *liking* stability?" she said. "That's just the way I am. I want a nice home, somewhere safe to go back to every night. Of course it would be perfect if there was a guy in the picture, but I'm not so needy that I'll take anything Devlin dishes out just because I've fallen for him all over again. I was his dishrag once. Not anymore. I have my limits, you know?"

"Unh."

*What were her limits?*

Law-breaking, for one. Lies, even lies by omission.

Then why had she been aiding and abetting a common criminal? Because he had actually kissed her senseless?

If that was the case, maybe she was way more needy than she'd been telling herself.

"But how come I'm not having stomach cramps?" she wondered out loud. "Every time I do something bad, I get sick with remorse. This time—nothing. Could it be that my gut knows something my head doesn't about Devlin Brandt?"

Wow. That was a thought!

The cab had reached her block, and she pointed out her building. While she took out her wallet, the cabbie leaned sideways and said, "I always tell my daughter she should listen to her heart. O'course, I got that from a romance novel."

Mackenzie blinked in surprise. In all her confessional cab rides, she'd never found a driver who'd offered a piece of advice. They usually just listened and nodded or grunted every once in a while. Half of them probably didn't know English in the first place. But this guy looked a little bit like an Irish gnome, with a plaid cap, pink cheeks and twinkly, currant eyes.

Was it...? *My gosh.* She'd finally come across the legendary prototype New York City cabbie—a kindly Irish chap who dispensed wisdom, wit and humor, all in the space of a few blocks' ride.

"Thank you," she said, stuffing a one-hundred-percent tip into his gnarled hand. "Thank you."

He tipped his hat.

Mackenzie found herself on the street, watching the yellow Checker cab pull away. The vehicle should have disappeared into the mist like Brigadoon, but instead it reached the blocked traffic at the intersection and blasted its horn for a full minute. She laughed. Proof enough for her. Definitely the prototype.

One of Mackenzie's neighbors was arriving home with her leashed dog, a fussy greyhound named Chin-Chin. They exchanged genialities and head pats. Mackenzie stayed back for a few seconds, checking the street for dinged-up Buicks. The only car that caught her attention was a big white Caddy, parked a couple doors down. The windows were tinted, but she could make out a lumpish silhouette in the back seat. The solitary figure gave her a shiver.

"Chin-Chin's been acting antsy tonight," the neighbor said as they entered the vestibule. The greyhound let out a sharp bark and pulled at the leash, his claws skittering over the tiles as he strained toward the door of Mackenzie's apartment.

Chin-Chin was always antsy, but Mackenzie smiled and nodded and gave the dog another pat. "Have a nice evening," she called as the neighbor urged her dog up the stairs.

Mackenzie stopped for her mail, then switched keys and approached her door, thinking about whether she should believe her heart, her head or her gut. All three couldn't be reliable—they seemed to be leading her in opposite directions.

The knob felt loose as she inserted the key. She tried it and the door swung open. Uh-oh.

The apartment was dark. It felt empty to her, but...disturbed. "Devlin?" she whispered, standing on the threshold.

She reached in and flicked on the hall light. The place appeared untouched from this vantage point.

She took her cell phone from her purse, ready to dial 9-1-1 at the first sign of a break-in, and edged into the hall. For a second she debated the options, but decided to shut the door behind her, locking only the push button on the knob so she could make a quick getaway if needed. It was possible she'd forgotten to lock up after Blair left this morning. Going out the back door had disrupted her usual routine, that's all.

"Hello," she said, taking a few steps. One glance into the kitchen was enough. Every cabinet and cupboard was open, with the contents strewn throughout the room. She looked to the right toward the living room—equally a disaster—and was checking for a signal on her phone when she saw the feet.

Male feet. Protruding from behind the sofa.

She screamed, "Devlin!" and dropped everything to fly over the debris of her living room.

"Please, God..." She dropped down beside the figure. Not Devlin. *Jason Dole.*

"Jason?" she cried. "Are you—"

She checked for a pulse, feeling around his cuffs and heavy wristwatch. Nothing. His neck was blocked by a stiff collar and knotted tie. She tore at them, pressing her finger to his carotid artery. Ah, there it was. A steady pulse.

"Thank heaven." There were no obvious signs of injury, just a lot of roses, strewn across his limp form. Her first thought was that he must have arrived with more flowers and surprised a burglar.

She pushed aside the question of Devlin and patted her old boyfriend's cheeks, hoping he would revive. "Jason? It's Mackenzie. Can you hear me?"

He groaned, eyelids fluttering.

"Don't move. I'm going to call for help."

Jason's hand gripped her when she started to rise. His head lifted. His lips moved. "Got her..."

She slipped her hands under his head and felt a large lump. "What, Jason? I don't—"

He made an unintelligible sound and closed his eyes again. His complexion was pasty, but there was still a good, strong heartbeat. Nonsensically, Mackenzie said, "Stay here," and went to find a phone.

The sight of her torn-apart apartment distracted her. Every drawer and shelf had been upended and swept clean. Vases were smashed, books thrown in heaps, the cushions of the sofa slashed to bits. It was sickening, but she had few items of important monetary value—

*Except the ring.*

She scrambled into the bedroom, meaning to take only two seconds. The jewelry box was open and her pearls were gone, but she didn't care. All she wanted was the ring.

She shoved her underwear drawer shut. The sock drawer below it also hung open, half the contents on the floor. The pair of white wool socks were easy to find, except that they were no longer paired. The intruder had torn them apart.

And taken the ring.

The limp, empty socks fell from her fingers. *Think of Jason,* she told herself, and abandoned the search. Snatching up the bedroom phone, she dialed the emergency number and gave the operator her address, explaining the situation as she returned to

Jason's supine form. He was moaning again, so she put the phone aside and tried to calm him.

The doorbell rang. Too soon to be an ambulance, so she approached it cautiously, checking the peephole. Blair's looming face filled the lens.

Mackenzie threw open the door. "My God, Blair! I need help. There's been a break-in and Jas—"

"I'm sorry," Blair cried out as she was propelled into the hallway, her head twisted at an awkward angle. Two men crowded in behind her, one of them holding Blair with his fist in her hair. "I heard Jason at your door and—"

"Shut up." The taller guy gave Blair's head a shake, and she winced in pain, tears running down her cheeks.

Mackenzie slowly backed away. She recognized both men as the pair who'd been hunting for Devlin. The gray-haired one was Sloss. The other was...

"I know you," she said, quite calmly considering how fast her heart was racing. "You're cops, right?"

Sloss laughed. "Sure, why not?"

"I'd like to interrogate *this* one," the younger guy said, slavering like a basset hound in Blair's ear. She whimpered.

"D-Devlin—" Mackenzie's voice broke, but she swallowed hard and spoke louder. "Devlin's not here."

"*Devlin's* not my first concern," Sloss said. He held a gun, pointing it first at Blair, then at Mackenzie. Casually, as if either one of them was expendable. "I want the ruby."

"I have no idea what you mean," Mackenzie said, cringing inside. She was a bad liar—the truth probably showed on her face.

The crags in Sloss's face deepened. "I say you do. We know Devil's been staying here. Saw him myself, and the redhead was persuaded to admit as much." Sloss advanced on Mackenzie, his heavy lids lowering to make slits of his dead eyes. "I bet I can get you to talk, too."

She gathered every shred of her bravado and narrowed her own eyes at him, pushing out her chin for good measure. "I suppose so. But it might take a while, and I've already called 9-1-1. The police and ambulance will be here any minute."

"Told you we shoulda grabbed her at the door," the second man said.

"I wanted to see if she'd run straight to a hiding spot." With the barrel of his gun, Sloss nudged Mackenzie's arms, then her hands. "Huh, girl? You got the ruby?"

She showed him her palms. "No. You already stole all my valuables—and I want them back. You have my grandmother's diamond ring."

"Bonny, did you take her grandmother's diamond ring?"

He chuckled. "Not me. Maybe Devil did."

"Tell you what," Sloss said, sliding so close to Mackenzie she could smell the heavy spice of his after-shave. "You lead me to the ruby, and I'll be nice in return. I'll make Devil give you back the ring."

Sirens wailed nearby. Although they were common in the city, Bonny reacted nervously. "We gotta get out of here," he said, wrenching Blair's head as he whirled toward the door. She cried out, clutching at her hair.

"All right," Mackenzie said. She couldn't let them take her and Blair, or worse, shoot them both dead on the spot. "I'll tell you where the ruby is, if you leave us alone."

Sloss smiled an arid smile. "I'll consider that. But first you talk. Where did Devil put the ruby?"

Mackenzie's mind was spinning through various scenarios as she tried to come up with a likely hiding place. The best idea that came to her was the one location, other than this apartment, where she and Devlin had been together.

He might yet come. He might rescue them.

She licked her lips and said, out of a last-ditch desperation, "My candy store, Sweet Something."

# 10

DEVLIN GOT LUCKY. He made one stop at his rented room in an Avenue B tenement—no use worrying anymore about whether or not it was being watched. The dingy room had been tossed, but they hadn't found his cache. He got down on his belly and reached past the dank underside of the clawfoot tub that sat against the kitchen wall, ripping away the package he'd duct-taped to the backside. It contained his shield and other ID, cell phone, weapon, ammo and cuffs. He was back in business.

From a cab, he placed a quick call to Jakes, who transferred to the precinct and learned that a police unit and ambulance had been dispatched to Mackenzie's address in Chelsea. For a moment, Devlin's world stopped—no sound, no motion, no life.

Then Jakes's voice returned, saying that an injured man was being removed from the apartment. There was no sign of Mackenzie, although one of the neighbors reported seeing her arrive home from work.

Devlin's luck still held—perhaps.

On a hunch, he told the cabbie to drop him in the Village. If there was no sign of Mackenzie at her store, he'd hunt Cheney down nonstop until he found her.

The Fat Man would regret his encounter with the Devil.

Most of the shops, galleries and cafés around Sweet Something had shut down for the night. There was still traffic and a number of pedestrians, enough that Devlin was covered as he got out of the cab and approached the candy emporium.

A gleaming white Caddy sat at the curb a short ways down. License plate—FAT MAN. Not exactly subtle, but when you were a four-hundred-pound crime kingpin with a grandiose ego and enough flashy jewelry hung on you to signal jet landings, subtle was not your watchword.

Devlin ducked behind a nearby car, assessing the situation.

Cheney sat in the back seat of the Caddy, as calm and rotund as a smiling Buddha. The lights were on inside Sweet Something. Steel mesh gates had been pulled across the windows, but Devlin glimpsed shapes moving back and forth inside.

He had a choice—make an arrest now, but risk alerting those inside, or let Cheney go and concentrate on rescuing Mack.

Not really a choice at all.

His cell phone was beeping, but he shut if off. Jakes would have his head for going in alone. Didn't matter. If he called for backup now, the N.Y.P.D. would roar in with sirens blaring and guns blazing, creating chaos from a situation that might yet be manageable.

Devlin checked the clip and slid his gun, shield and

cuffs into the back of his jeans, sliding Blair's fanny pad around to the back for cover. He stripped off his top shirt and peeled away the bandanna, wadding them up with the phone and leaving them in the gutter. Although the cover they provided was flimsy, he waited for a group of pedestrians to pass by before rising and sprinting to the front door of Sweet Something. Cheney might have spotted him, but that couldn't be helped.

Devlin had planned to shoot his way inside if it was absolutely necessary. The glass door was open. Another lucky break. He could see Sloss inside, waving a gun in the air. Mackenzie was gesturing at the portholes and candy bins.

Devlin said a short prayer, pushed open the door and strolled into the store as casually as if he'd come to buy a bag of Gobstoppers.

"I SWEAR I DON'T know *where* Devlin hid the ruby," Mackenzie said. Sloss was getting increasingly agitated. She sidled closer to Blair, who'd finally been released by the man she'd learned was called Bonaventure aka "Bonny." On the ride to Sweet Something, Mackenzie and Blair had sat on either side of a large bald man in the back seat of the white Cadillac she'd noticed parked outside her building, with Sloss and his partner Bonaventure in the front.

With a certain flair, the large man had introduced himself as Boris Cheney, their host. Their *host!* Mackenzie and Blair had exchanged a look, but they'd kept their mouths shut. Cheney had then introduced his employees, and begun chatting as if they were on a pleasant Sunday drive. He spoke of the price of real estate in Manhattan. Of his aversion to city grit and grime. He preferred the suburbs, he said, and had expanded his business into upstate New York for that purpose. "Less concrete and more lawn—that's what we all need," he'd purred, rubbing a heavy gold cabochon ruby pinky ring across his bulbous midsection.

"Forest Lawn," Bonaventure had said from the front, casting an oily grin at Mackenzie and Blair. He'd seemed to relish the thought of sending them six feet under the sod at the well-known suburban cemetery.

Now Sloss was pacing around Sweet Something, staring in astonishment at the silver pipes and neon tubes. He kicked one of the Lucite chairs, sending it crashing to the floor. "If the ruby's not in the safe," he barked, "where is it?" He pointed his gun at Mackenzie. "You. Get over here. Tell me where it is or I'll have you empty every hard candy in this place onto the floor."

Blair gave Mackenzie's hand a squeeze.

She moved toward the candy counter, waving at the bins helplessly. At their arrival, she'd taken Sloss into the back room and opened the small wall safe to prove that the ruby he was after wasn't stashed inside.

"It could be anywhere." She unlatched one of the portholes and stuck her hand inside, sifting through the candy. For a fleeting moment, she wondered if she and Blair would get a chance to run if she distracted Sloss by pelting him with lemon drops.

A new voice spoke. "I'll show you where the ruby is."

Mackenzie gasped. *Devlin!*

Sloss leveled his gun at Devlin's midsection. "Well, well, what have we here?"

Bonaventure had grabbed Blair again. He spoke from behind her, taunting Devlin. "Aren't you the pretty one?"

*What a weasel*, Mackenzie thought.

"Frisk him," Sloss said.

Bonaventure blanched, but he went over to Devlin and started patting him down. Devlin winked. "You're not afraid to touch me, are you, Bonny Rabbit?"

"Don't call me that," Bonaventure spat. His face had turned a dull red. "You're the pansy. Look at your shirt."

"The jewels are fake, but I still like it."

Bonaventure slid a hand down Devlin's leg, barely grazing him. Mackenzie could see what Devlin was doing—making the other man wary of getting too close. She didn't know why, exactly, but she had a suspicion that he was armed in some way.

"Fruitcake," Bonny said, switching to the other leg. He reached Devlin's rear end and paused before giving it a tentative poke. "Hey, Sloss—there's something in here."

"Oh!" Devlin laughed. "That's just my fanny pad."

Bonaventure had started to reach inside the waist-band of Devlin's jeans, but the explanation made him pull back in disgust.

"Here you go." Devlin pulled out the pad and tossed it on the floor.

Bonaventure recoiled. "Ugh. I need to wash my hands."

"Don't be an idiot," Sloss said. "He's playing with you."

Devlin smiled, giving Bonny the eye. "That's right."

Bonaventure backed away.

"Quit with the games, Devil—Devlin—whatever your name is." Sloss approached him, but stayed well back. "Give me the ruby you swiped from the boss and we'll be on our way."

"Sure you will."

Sloss blinked, glancing from Blair to Mackenzie and back to Devlin. "Got any other ideas, fancy pants?"

Devlin shrugged. "All right. You can have the ruby."

"Thatta girl. Lead me to it." Sloss waved Devlin further into the store. "Bonny, keep an eye on these two. Devil tries anything, you know what to do."

Bonny slid his hand around Blair's neck. He pulled her body up against his. "Sure do."

Devlin stared hard at Mackenzie as he walked by, but she didn't know what he wanted her to do. Disable Bonaventure if given the chance, she imagined. But with what? Atomic Fireballs? A licorice whip?

"It's upstairs," Devlin said, and she began to wonder if he'd actually stashed the ruby at Sweet Something.

Sloss followed him up the spiral staircase, heavy footfalls making the metal clang.

Devlin pointed at one of the candy columns. "In here."

"What the hell?" Sloss gaped at the tower of red jawbreakers. "Where?"

"Somewhere in there. I dropped it inside from the hatch on top. It could have sifted halfway down by now."

"Son of a bitch. You'd better not be conning me."

Mackenzie had tilted her face upward, following them across the balcony. Devlin was telling the truth, she realized, remembering the first day he'd come to the store and she'd given him the fifty-cent tour. He'd been interested in the columns. Then she'd gone into her office and when she came out, the hatch had been opened and he'd been pulling on his boot.

*His boot*, she thought. How odd. Had he been carrying a stolen ruby in his boot all this time?

Well, why not? She had kept a diamond ring in her socks. And now one of the goons had it....

Sloss leaned over the railing. "Bonny, you and the girls look for it from down there. Start emptying this thing if you have to."

"That won't work," Mackenzie said. "We'd need too many quarters."

"It's like a giant gum ball machine," Bonny called.

Sloss had motioned for Devlin to flip the hatch.

Mackenzie glimpsed his grim face as he leaned over the railing and thrust his arms into the jawbreakers, fishing around for the ruby.

It didn't take Sloss long to realize how futile the effort was. "We need a bucket."

Bonaventure was holding his gun carelessly as he fed spare change into the slot at the base of the column, cranking out another jawbreaker with each coin. He let them spill out, one by one. Thoughtfully, Mackenzie watched them roll across the hard tile floor.

Sloss had grabbed the mail basket from Mackenzie's office and given it to Devlin. He shoveled it full of jawbreakers, then emptied them on the floor. Sloss swiped the candies away from the balcony with the side of his foot. The jawbreakers rolled willy-nilly in all directions, some of them dropping to the first floor with a sharp *crack.*

"I think I have it," Devlin said. He was halfway over the railing, gripping it with one hand as he stretched to reach as far as he could into the tower of jawbreakers.

Sloss leaned in for a closer look.

Devlin strained. "Can't...reach..."

Mackenzie took a couple steps back, trying for a better view. She knew she had to be ready to act when Devlin made his move.

He pulled out. "Sorry, I didn't get it. The ruby's in there. Just out of reach."

"I'll do it." Sloss shoved Devlin aside. He scowled, warning him with a flip of his gun. "Don't try anything or both you and your kinky girlfriends buy it. Bonny—you watching them?"

Bonaventure glanced over his shoulder at Mackenzie and Blair, who huddled together, apparently as nonthreatening as baby mice. "Yeah, sure."

Mackenzie touched Blair's arm, trying to send a signal with her eyes as Sloss reached into the jawbreakers, stirring them about as his arm thrust deeper. Devlin peered sideways into the Plexiglas tower, urging the other man on. "It's there...a few more inches... keep trying—"

"Argh!" Sloss suddenly yelled.

Mackenzie glanced up. Devlin had shoved Sloss into the jawbreakers face first. The man was flailing, but with his head and arms stuck inside the wide column there wasn't much he could do.

A loud *pop* shook the column. Devlin shouted at the same moment.

At first Mackenzie thought the column had cracked. But the alarm in Devlin's voice made her realize that Sloss had fired his gun into the jawbreakers.

Bonaventure jumped away from the column. One foot landed on the candies he'd spilled. He lost his balance, falling with a *crack* on an elbow. The blow jarred the gun out of his hand. It slid a couple of feet across the floor.

Mackenzie and Blair scrambled for it, but so did Bonaventure. He launched himself, ending up atop them just as Blair reached the gun. Mackenzie's breath was knocked out of her. She felt bodies squirming, heard Blair cry out—

"Bitch!" Bonaventure had one of his hands on the gun, over Blair's. With the other he slammed her face into the floor.

"Police!" Devlin shouted from the balcony. "Freeze!"

All three of them looked up. Sloss was now handcuffed to the railing, spitting and swearing. Devlin was coming down the steps, both hands locked on the gun he had leveled at Bonaventure. "Blair, Mackenzie, get out of the way...."

Mackenzie pushed back, sliding on her rump. Blair was too entangled with the crook to move. When Bonaventure realized that, he snaked an arm around her waist. He twisted to his side, using Blair as a shield.

"Don't move!" Devlin barked from the bottom of the staircase.

"You wouldn't shoot a woman," Bonaventure said, still grappling for the gun. Blair looked woozy, but she was hanging on.

"Yeah?" Devlin sneered. "Well, this one's a drag queen. In other words, she's a man."

Bonaventure, startled to be trapped in an intimate horizontal hug with a drag queen, froze for a fraction of a second.

Immediately Devlin stepped in and stomped a boot on the thug's wrist. He also clipped Blair, but she had the presence of mind to fling the gun out of reach as her fingers flew open and her wrists flattened to the floor.

"Sorry," Devlin said to her, bending over and jabbing his knee between Bonaventure's shoulder blades. In an appropriate payback for the way he'd manhandled Blair, Devlin gave the back of Bonaventure's skull a hard shove, thunking his forehead on the tiles. "Stay down and keep down, Bonny."

A sobbing Blair rolled away and threw herself into Mackenzie's arms. Mackenzie automatically comforted her friend, but she was also staring up at Devlin in astonishment. "You're a cop?"

"Yes." Though his eyes flicked at her, he was all business, maintaining his position over Bonaventure as sirens screamed out on the street. Brakes squealed. Lights strobed through the iron-gated windows.

"I don't believe it," Mackenzie didn't, even though it made a strange sort of sense. His phrase "make a case" had been nagging at her, but there'd been nothing in his actions or emotions that suggested what she perceived as a cop's mentality.

"I'd show you my shield, but I'm afraid it slid down the back of my jeans when I pulled out the cuffs for Sloss."

"Then that's *your* gun."

He smiled. "I hid it under the fanny pad. Good costume, Blair."

Blair let out a watery laugh. "You do know that I'm a woman, don't you?" she asked as if she were insulted, holding her injured wrist to her chest.

Devlin never got to answer. The front doors of Sweet Something banged open and police officers poured into the room, guns cocked. Devlin clicked the safety on his weapon and put up his hands as they descended on him and Bonaventure.

He was shouting that he was a cop. And that was the last that Mackenzie heard from him.

BLAIR WAS SENT to the hospital for X rays of her right wrist and evaluation of her head trauma. Mackenzie went along, accompanied by a couple of police detectives who questioned her thoroughly in an empty waiting room. She told them everything—from Devlin's appearance on her doorstep to a detailed account of the incident at Sweet Something. They refused to confirm that Devlin was a cop, but she sensed that it was so.

She was too tired and sore to concentrate on how she felt about that. Most of her thoughts were centered on Blair, although she remembered to check on Jason's status. A nurse told her he'd been knocked unconscious but was recovering nicely. Mackenzie was brought in to speak briefly with him, apologizing out of guilt and getting a quick version of his side of the story. Jason looked at Mackenzie with some alarm as she explained about Devlin, and she knew that she'd probably seen the last of her ex. Jason was dogged, but not a risk-taker by any means. It was strange for her to realize that her life had become an adventure.

Finally a doctor came out and said that Blair had a

wrist sprain and a mild concussion. Nothing serious, but she was to be kept in the hospital overnight for observation.

After a few words of comfort, Mackenzie was driven home by a kindly police officer who even came inside to turn on lights and check the rooms. When the cop saw the state of the apartment—the police had already been there to gather evidence—he offered to bring her to a hotel or to friends or family. Mackenzie's parents lived too far away and when she thought of having to tell Sabrina what had happened to the ring and ruining Kit's proposal, it was all she could do not to burst into tears.

She would stay here, she told the cop, thanking him profusely. She locked the door and made a wan tour of the wrecked rooms, feeling heartsick as she shoved items back in place and swept up broken glass. Her apartment was no longer her haven. But it hadn't been, not to its original extent, ever since Devlin had arrived and blown her contentment to smithereens.

Yeah, she'd wanted to change her life and she had—in spades. Or *he* had.

After a cup of tea and a quick bite that went down like lead, she took a hot bath, trying not to think about the fate of the diamond ring and, even less successfully, not to think about Devlin.

He wasn't a thief. He was a cop.

It was like discovering that a pig could fly. Or that a dog could talk. Or that a devil had sprouted angel's wings and was hovering over her bathtub, flapping his wings and winking a mischievous eye.

"Snap out of it," she said, climbing out of the tepid water.

She dried herself, picked up the clothing that had been strewn around the bedroom, found a sleep shirt and went to bed. *Blissfully Single* fell to the floor with a thud when she flung back the blankets.

Blissfully single? Blessedly alone. She was lucky, after all. She'd survived a break-in and a kidnapping. So what if she'd lost a lover along the way?

Mackenzie closed her eyes, wishing she could sleep. Devlin hadn't given her a glance after the N.Y.P.D. had arrived. He'd been all business. While Sloss and Bonaventure were removed in handcuffs and the guns recovered and the search for the ruby begun—apparently it *was* hidden somewhere among her jawbreakers—Devlin had been held outside, the center of several heated exchanges before he'd abruptly taken off into the night. She had no idea where he'd gone, and wasn't sure that she even *wanted* to know.

Pigs were flying, dogs were yakking...

And her guardian devil had left her on her own.

DEVLIN WAS a burglar again.

He'd come to steal Mackenzie's heart.

He hadn't let himself focus on her in those frenzied moments when he'd drawn his weapon on Sloss, leaving her and Blair at Bonny's mercy for a few precious seconds that might have led to tragedy if they hadn't been such fighters.

His heart had nearly stopped when they'd been wrestling Bonaventure for the gun. If he'd had a clean shot at Bonny, he'd have taken it without remorse, but he was glad it hadn't come to that. Shooting someone he'd "befriended," even as a charade, would have put a traumatic end to his career as an undercover cop. As it was, he'd finished well. Not smartly or by the book, as Jakes had pointed out rather forcefully, but well.

Still, he wasn't feeling the triumph he'd expected.

Little wonder. After running on adrenaline for the past several hours, he was now crashing fast. Sand coated his eyeballs and weighted his lids. Every muscle was lax with exhaustion. But something greater than fatigue or even justice well done had driven him to Mackenzie's back door.

Something he had to finish. Now, before morning light.

Quietly, he let himself inside. The bedroom wasn't dark this time. Lights were on in the hallway and bathroom. He knew about the break-in, but the room wasn't in great disarray so she must have cleaned up. That was his Mack.

He thought briefly of leaving the item he'd taken at risk of yet another departmental reprimand. But that was the coward's way out. When he was seventeen and full of false bravado, he hadn't fully recognized what he had in Mackenzie, either as a friend or a potential girlfriend. Now, he knew better. And he hoped he was man enough to match her.

Of their own volition, his eyes sought her out…only to find her sitting up in bed, watching his every move. Her knees were drawn up, her hands resting atop them. "I'm awake," she said.

At the sound of her voice, some of the tension left him. She was so accepting, so warmhearted. "Were you expecting me?"

"No. Not at all."

"Ah."

"I thought I'd seen the last of you, now that my usefulness was gone."

Maybe not so accepting. He'd have to tread carefully.

Yet he smiled to himself, his belief in her not shaken. No matter. He was trained to tread carefully, and she did deserve an explanation.

He approached the bed, but didn't sit, even though he yearned to feel her soft body curving into his. "I never meant to use you…."

She snorted.

"I know—I did. I used you, the same way I've used every contact I've made in the past few months working this case. What can I say? I'm sorry, but I had a job to do regardless of my feelings for you."

She exhaled, her head drooping to touch her upraised knees. "You have feelings for me?" Her voice was muffled.

"I've lied about most everything else in my life, but

not that." He lowered himself to the bed, and when she didn't react he slid closer, propping his hands on the either side of the headboard behind her, leaning in so close he could smell the soap on her skin, but still wasn't *quite* touching her. He breathed her scent, her warmth. She was a balm and an intoxicant and an everlasting flame. "I love you, Mack."

Her face lifted, revealing glistening eyes. "I don't know you, Devlin."

He touched her soft mouth with a gliding kiss. "You do."

"No." Her lips parted slightly, giving him the velvet brush of her tongue. "You're here, you've been here, in my bed, and I don't know you."

His fingers tightened on the headboard, holding him back from taking her in a sweeping embrace. *Tread carefully.* "We'll start now, then. I'll tell you everything."

Her hand hovered near his cheek as if she didn't dare touch him. Her eyes searched his. "This might be a dream."

"Nope. Flesh and blood." He kissed her again, flexing his shoulders and bending his elbows to push more firmly against her.

She caught her breath and put her hands to his chest, steadying him, not ready to concede. "We need to get the facts straight before this goes any further."

"You're right. How's Blair? I'm sorry if I hurt her—"

"Don't worry. That couldn't be helped. She's going

to be fine—a sprain and a concussion from when that creep slammed her head on the floor." Mackenzie shuddered.

"And the other guy—your old boyfriend?"

"Jason Dole. He'll be okay too, but he's definitely an ex now." She tried to make light of it, but Devlin could tell how traumatic the evening had been. "Finally scared him off for good."

"How did Jason happen onto the scene?"

"From what I pieced together, he arrived with flowers for me and Blair buzzed him in. She has my keys, so they were going into my apartment to leave the flowers and interrupted those—those—"

"Arthur Sloss and Kip 'Bonny' Bonaventure."

"You're far too kind. They don't deserve polite names. Anyway, one of them knocked out Jason. They nabbed Blair and forced her back to her own apartment to wait for me to come home."

"Why? Hadn't they already searched your place?"

"I guess they were hoping I had a better hiding place than the toe of my socks." She narrowed her eyes. "Or the toe of your boot."

"You figured that out, huh?"

"Why'd you put the ruby in the jawbreakers?"

"Because it was the last place I thought of. Normally I make arrangements with my supervisor to drop off evidence as I accumulate it, but with Sloss and Bonny hippity-hopping hot on my trail, that was too big a risk."

"But *Sweet Something?* You could have gotten a

locker at the bus station or even a safety deposit box. Anything."

"Maybe so, but I was in emergency mode. And thinking like my alter ego more than law enforcement. We call it going native, when you've been undercover too long. The strangest things begin to make sense, and usually you get pretty damn paranoid."

"I see."

She didn't. He didn't want her to, either. He'd lived too long as one of the dregs of society and none of that should have ever in a million years touched Mackenzie. It would take him a long time to forgive himself for involving her, however desperate or crazy he'd been.

"How did you all end up at Sweet Something?" he asked.

"I pulled that out of my hat," she said. "Maybe I suspected you of *something*, now that I'm looking at it with hindsight. I told the gray-haired guy that the ruby was hidden at my candy store. At worst, I thought it would give me and Blair a chance to get away or...give *you* a chance to find us."

"Thank God I did."

She squeezed his leg. "Yes. You were so clever, about hiding the gun, and the disguise. Freaked them both out."

"You and Blair were incredible."

"Scared, you mean."

"And brave."

She sighed. "I realize that it's police business, but

can you explain about the case? Who was the man in the Cadillac?''

"Keep this to yourself, okay?'' She nodded. "That was the boss—the big arrest we were after. Boris Cheney, known on the street as the Fat Man. He owns half a dozen pawnshops in the city and suburbs, running stolen goods through them. Three months ago I was assigned to the case. I worked my way into the fringes of the theft ring that supplies Cheney. A couple of days before you and I met again, there'd been a heist. The ruby was part of the haul—an extremely identifiable piece. I was studying it in the back room of one of Cheney's shops when Bonaventure found me. He jumped to the conclusion that I was trying to rip them off. So I got a little beat up—''

"A little," Mackenzie said in a shaky voice.

"I never carry ID, so they didn't think I was a cop. But I had slipped the ruby into my boot and when Cheney learned it was missing he sent down orders that Sloss had better find it and take care of me.''

"Take care? I have another definition of that phrase.''

"Shh.'' He stroked her hair, relaxing himself more than her. "It's over now. Don't worry.''

Mackenzie was still thinking about the case. "Did Cheney get away?''

"Nope.''

"That's why you disappeared so fast.''

"Yep. It wasn't too tough tracking down a huge, bejeweled bald man wedged behind the wheel of a white

Cadillac. One of our units ran him down on his way north."

"So it's over?"

There was much to come, but Devlin said yes.

"Will I have to testify?"

"Probably, unless they all cop pleas. It won't be so bad, Mack. I'll be with you."

"Promise?"

"If you let me."

She wasn't quite there. "I'll think about it. But first you have to tell me what happened to you. I want to know how you became a cop in the first place."

"It wasn't an overnight decision. I can't list the reasons for you. All I can say is that I'd reached a point where it was either go straight or go bad. For once in my life, I made the right choice."

She shook her head. "I can't quite comprehend it. You made such a good hoodlum."

"Exactly. That's how I got into undercover work. They like to pick raw kids right out of the academy because they don't act like cops yet."

"Then you've been doing this for...?"

"Six years. On various cases. I've been in deep cover. That means I live, eat and sleep my street identity, with very little contact from the department. It's not a lifestyle that makes for a healthy mental outlook. Very...lonely."

She rubbed his shoulder. "What about the prison record? How could you become a police officer when—"

"That's not legit. Just another detail of my false identity as 'Devil' Brandt. I *did* go to prison, but only long enough to set up a rock-solid background."

"But everyone believes it!"

"They're supposed to."

"Even your parents?"

"They know the truth, but can't talk about it."

"That's a terrible thing to ask of them, Devlin. Parents want to be proud of their son's accomplishments."

"Most do, I suppose. But we were never that close anyway. You know a little about the problems there...." He shrugged. "They're private people, they live quietly. It's not as if they're outgoing or even very sociable and are constantly having to explain about their criminal son...."

"Even so."

He swallowed the lump that had formed in his throat. "If it matters, that's over now."

She made a quizzical sound.

"I'm out of it. This job was my last undercover assignment. I told Jakes tonight. He's my supervisor, what we call a cutout. My contact, you know? He didn't even try to talk me out of it, so maybe he already knew I was burned-out on cover work."

Her breathing became audible. "Are you sure?"

"Absolutely. I want a *real* life."

"Real..."

"With you, Mackenzie." He chuckled, a roughened, scratchy sound that hurt his throat.

"But I—"

"Yeah, yeah, you don't know me," he said. "That's not completely true. You know me better than anyone, I think." Perhaps that was a sad commentary on his previous life, but there was no reason for him not to start new. Goodbye, Devil.

*Hello, Mack.*

He dropped his hands to her waist and held his face on a level with her gaze. "Hello."

"Hi." Her smile was both shy and sexy—pure Mackenzie.

"Would you like to go out to dinner with me?"

"When?"

"Not immediately. I have debriefing. A case to work on, adjustments to make. But I'll be back, as soon as I can. If you're willing to wait…"

She spoke quickly, saying, "It's a date," with a certain gravity. And then she laughed.

He laughed, too. Mack was an amazing woman.

He found her mouth again, tightened his hands on her waist. She stretched out her legs, molding to him as they slid lower on the bed. "Meanwhile," he said, feathering her with kisses, "can I sleep with you tonight?"

"Hmm. You, I don't know about. But Devil, now—*that* man can talk me into just about anything…."

He'd have to keep that in mind. "There's one more thing."

"Oh?"

"Give me your hand."

She did, so trustingly his heart nearly burst.

"The other one," he whispered, reaching into the pocket of his grungy jeans.

He played with her fingers for a little bit, stroking them one by one, kissing her palm, nibbling the tips. Somewhere in there, he slipped the diamond ring on her third finger.

She inhaled. "Devlin?"

"I heard they stole this from you. It's evidence, of course. Officially, you can't have it back yet. But I don't always follow the rules." He lifted her hand toward the light. "This time, maybe you're glad of that?"

"Very much," she said in a choked voice. Suddenly she was hugging him, half-laughing, half-crying. "Thank you, thank you. I was afraid the ring was gone for good, and Kit is proposing to Sabrina tomorrow and it wouldn't be the same for her if he didn't have the ring and I would have felt so terrible...." She held her hand up again to admire the ring. "Thank you, Devlin."

"You're giving it to Sabrina?"

"Uh-huh."

"Okay."

She examined his expression. "Something wrong with that? Oh, you mean because it's evidence? Can't we keep it for at least a few days...please? I don't want to explain to Sabrina until after tomorrow. She should have her day, untainted."

"I'll fix it so you can keep it, yeah."

"Sabrina will be so happy."

"What about you?"

Mackenzie's eyes widened. "I'm not getting engaged."

"Not yet, no. You barely know me, after all." He pressed his palm against hers, then folded their fingers together, saving every dream of what might be between their clasped hands. "But there's always tomorrow, sugar."

# ____ **Epilogue** ____

*Eight months later*

"I SIMPLY DON'T understand it!" Nicole Bliss said from one end of the long mahogany table in her elegant, candlelighted dining room. Mackenzie and Sabrina had wanted to hold their parents' anniversary party at Decadence or Sweet Something, but Nicole insisted that they should have a family affair in their own Scarsdale home.

"What's the problem now?" Charlie Bliss rolled his eyes with what had become his usual bemused tolerance of his outspoken wife.

Nicole looked at him and smiled, reminded by his teasing to soften her approach. "Eight months ago, all I heard from our daughters was talk of proposals and engagement rings. And now here we are after all this time—" she looked at both daughters "—and neither one of you is married yet!"

Sabrina tossed her sun-bleached hair. "Don't rush me. Kit and I are only just back from Bermuda. We haven't had time to think about planning a wedding."

"Kristoffer," Nicole said, "you need to hurry your fiancée along."

"Ah, but we're really enjoying our engagement." Kit looked at Sabrina with a sly grin, before picking up her hand and kissing the top of it. With his black hair, deep tan, gold earring and loose white cotton shirt, he looked more than ever like a pirate. Sabrina and he had indulged in several delectable fantasies during their months on the high seas, but now that they were back they planned to settle down for a while, resuming their jobs at Decadence.

Nicole sighed and turned to Mackenzie and Devlin, seated on the other side of the table. "Well?"

Mackenzie blushed. "Mom!"

She didn't look at Devlin. He was a detective in the robbery division now, having gone through several strenuous months when he'd been both testifying at Cheney's trial and adjusting to a normal life without secrets and lies. For a time, their relationship had been touch and go, but now they'd been dating seriously since Christmas, when Mackenzie had been instrumental in reuniting him with his parents.

Devlin took her hand under cover of the tablecloth. "She keeps promising to make an honest man of me, but…" He shrugged.

Sabrina slipped off the heirloom engagement

ring and tossed it across the table to Mackenzie. "Dare you!"

Mackenzie caught it out of pure reflex. "Sabrina, I'm not—this is—"

"We never did settle the bet, did we?"

"What bet?" Nicole asked.

Sabrina laughed. "It's private. Just between sisters."

"Not anymore," Mackenzie said with a groan. She held the ring between two fingers, fighting the urge to try it on.

"Both of us did very well, I'd say." Sabrina glanced first at Kit, then at Devlin. He'd cleaned up quite well from what Mackenzie sometimes called his "thief of hearts" days. "We could always share the ring."

Mackenzie shook her head. "No, I want you to have it." She'd insisted on that because the ring really did mean more to Sabrina than to her. Maybe because it was the only thing—other than Kit—that roused Sabrina's soft, sentimental side.

"How about if I make it a loaner?" Sabrina winked at Devlin. "Just so you two can do the official engagement thing."

"Oh, no…" Mackenzie tried not to sound flustered, but her heart was pounding like crazy.

Devlin let go of her hand.

She swallowed with disappointment, then realized that he'd set aside the napkin in his lap and had nudged his chair back to give him room to go down on one knee. "Mackenzie?"

She could hardly see him for blinking. "Devlin?"

"I put this ring on you once before," he said, plucking it from her boneless fingers. "Remember?"

"Of course," she breathed.

He toyed with her fingers the way he had on that unforgettable night in her bedroom when she'd thought they were over before discovering that they were just beginning.

Charlie, Nicole, Sabrina and Kit all rose out of their chairs, craning their necks to see. Mackenzie squeezed her eyes shut. When she opened them, the ring was on her finger and Devlin was looking at her expectantly. "Well?"

"Devil," she said.

He smiled. "Sweet angel."

Mackenzie looked up at Sabrina, who nodded, her eyes welling. *Go on! Change your life.*

The words that would do so once more filled Mackenzie's head before she opened her mouth and let them out. She couldn't tell if she was whispering or shouting. All she knew was that she said them.

"Will you marry me?"

And then there was the cheering and applause and Devlin with his strong arms around her and his mouth at her ear. Devlin, saying "Yes."

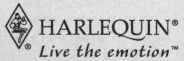

# HARLEQUIN®
## Temptation.

# AMERICAN HEROES

### These men are heroes—
### strong, fearless...
### And impossible to resist!

Join bestselling authors Lori Foster, Donna Kauffman
and Jill Shalvis as they deliver up

# MEN OF COURAGE

**Harlequin anthology
May 2003**

Followed by *American Heroes* miniseries
in Harlequin Temptation

**RILEY by Lori Foster
June 2003**

**SEAN by Donna Kauffman
July 2003**

**LUKE by Jill Shalvis
August 2003**

Don't miss this sexy new miniseries by some of
Temptation's hottest authors!

*Available at your favorite retail outlet.*

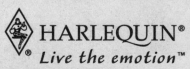

# HARLEQUIN®
## *Live the emotion*™

**Visit us at www.eHarlequin.com**

HTAH

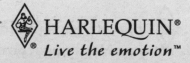

If you enjoyed what you just read,
then we've got an offer you can't resist!

# Take 2 bestselling love stories FREE!

# Plus get a FREE surprise gift!

---

**Clip this page and mail it to Harlequin Reader Service®**

| **IN U.S.A.** | **IN CANADA** |
|---|---|
| 3010 Walden Ave. | P.O. Box 609 |
| P.O. Box 1867 | Fort Erie, Ontario |
| Buffalo, N.Y. 14240-1867 | L2A 5X3 |

**YES!** Please send me 2 free Harlequin Temptation® novels and my free surprise gift. After receiving them, if I don't wish to receive anymore, I can return the shipping statement marked cancel. If I don't cancel, I will receive 4 brand-new novels each month, before they're available in stores. In the U.S.A., bill me at the bargain price of $3.57 plus 25¢ shipping and handling per book and applicable sales tax, if any*. In Canada, bill me at the bargain price of $4.24 plus 25¢ shipping and handling per book and applicable taxes**. That's the complete price and a savings of 10% off the cover prices—what a great deal! I understand that accepting the 2 free books and gift places me under no obligation ever to buy any books. I can always return a shipment and cancel at any time. Even if I never buy another book from Harlequin, the 2 free books and gift are mine to keep forever.

142 HDN DNT5
342 HDN DNT6

| Name | (PLEASE PRINT) | |
|---|---|---|
| Address | Apt.# | |
| City | State/Prov. | Zip/Postal Code |

 * Terms and prices subject to change without notice. Sales tax applicable in N.Y.
 ** Canadian residents will be charged applicable provincial taxes and GST.
 All orders subject to approval. Offer limited to one per household and not valid to
 current Harlequin Temptation® subscribers.
 ® are registered trademarks of Harlequin Enterprises Limited.

TEMP02                                    ©1998 Harlequin Enterprises Limited